Back From the Dead

AE Moran

Invisible Publishing Company

Contents

Chapter 1: Caroline

"**M**ommy! I want Mommy!" My two-year-old son Dylan raises his arms above his head and jumps up and down.

I laugh and kiss him for the thousandth time. "I love you, sweetie. You're going to have a great day. I'll see you this afternoon when I come to pick you up after work."

"Mommy!" he yells. "I want Mommy!"

My best friend Willow Hastings steps in. "Hey, Dylan. We just made a brand-new batch of play dough. Some of the other kids are already playing with it. Why don't you go over to the table and see?"

She turns him around so he's facing the play dough table and gives him a push to propel him across the room. He takes a few halting steps, and in that moment's pause, he sees the other kids kneading and rolling bright green play dough on the table.

He keeps walking and I take the opening to escape. I hug Willow. "Thanks. I owe you big time. You're a lifesaver."

"It's my secret superpower." She waves me toward the street where my car sits parked at the curb. "Get out of here while you can."

I laugh and turn away. Willow is already hanging up Dylan's coat and backpack on the hooks by the door. She really is a lifesaver and she's the best with kids.

I start to leave when I stop dead in my tracks and gasp in horror. "Oh, my God!"

Willow looks up. "What's wrong?"

I can't move. I stand riveted to the spot and ice water dumps into my veins.

Willow follows my gaze and she gasps, too. "Oh, my God!"

We both stand there staring in abject shock at a man standing across the street. He wears a thick leather bomber jacket that shows off his muscular shoulders, faded jeans, and tan work boots.

His short-clipped black-brown hair hangs over his forehead and frames his rugged features, but it's those crystal black eyes that make my world tilt on its axis. I would recognize those eyes anywhere.

"It can't be him," Willow mutters. "It just can't be."

I shake my head, but I can't make a sound. My throat feels parched and I can't decide whether to run away or attack someone.

Willow swivels in front of me and blocks my view of him. "Caroline! Look at me! It isn't him, okay? Your husband died in an explosion in the Philippines five years ago. That can't be Hunter. It just can't be."

"I.... I know. It's just....they never found the body.....It might be...."

"It isn't," she snaps, but she glances over her shoulder at the man like she's just as afraid of him as I am.

He stands there staring right at me. Why would he do that if he isn't Hunter? Is this really my long-dead husband coming back from beyond the grave?

Willow plants herself in front of my eyes and commands my full attention while she whispers low in my face. "Listen to me, Caroline.

Hunter loved you more than anything. He worshiped the ground you walk on. If there was the slightest chance that he survived that explosion, he would have come back a long time ago. He wouldn't be showing up now after five years gone. You know that. He didn't just come back all of a sudden. He's dead. This is some other guy."

I nod fast. I want more than anything to believe that, but....

Willow massages both my shoulders. "You need to get to work or you'll be late. Go get in your car and drive to your office. Don't look at that guy again. Understand?"

I nod again, but I can't move. Cold sweat breaks out all over my body. What if it is Hunter? Why would he stand over there staring at me instead of coming over to talk to me? Why would he come back to town without telling me?

"You did the right thing by getting pregnant with Dylan," Willow goes on. "You had to rebuild your life after Hunter died and you did that by having the child you always wanted. So what if you used donor sperm to get pregnant? You're the mother of a beautiful little boy and you're a great mother. You have nothing to be ashamed of. Even if Hunter came back—which he won't—he would be proud of you. You have no reason to think he would mind that you had Dylan now."

I nod again. I don't seem to be able to stop myself. I can't do anything else. "O...okay. I know you're right. I just have to...."

I glance toward my car planning how I'm going to get there without the guy seeing me, but when Willow follows my gaze again, we both see that the guy is gone. He's nowhere in sight and I nearly collapse in shaky relief.

I pass my hand across my eyes. "I don't think I can take this."

"It's okay," Willow tells me. "It isn't Hunter. You understand that, don't you? Hunter is dead."

"Yeah," I gasp. "I know."

"Go on and get to work. Whoever that guy is, he won't hurt you."

I nod one last time, she pats me on the back, and I start walking to my car. Thank God the guy isn't there anymore because there is no way in Hell I could walk to my car with him watching me.

Is it Hunter after all? This guy looks exactly like Hunter. He has the same build, the same hair, the same chiseled features, the same eyes—oh, my God—those eyes!

I shiver when I turn the ignition, put my car in gear, and drive away. Seeing those eyes bring back so many memories that they overwhelm my mind.

Willow is right. Hunter and I were madly, world-shatteringly in love....and then I got the call that he had been killed in an explosion while he was deployed in the Philippines.

That one phone call flattened my whole world. It took me two years to get over losing him.....except that I didn't get over him. I missed him and cried for him just as much after two years as I did after two days.

Only Dylan pulled me out of it. I had to move on. I had to start planning my future without Hunter in it and that meant having children. I couldn't count on meeting another guy who made me feel the way Hunter did.

So I used donor sperm and got pregnant. Now I have the life of my dreams, a good job, and a son who fills my life with love. I don't want anything else....so why is Hunter coming back to haunt me now?

He isn't. This isn't Hunter. It can't be. Hunter's dead, but the doubts and questions still nag me. What if......?

What if he somehow survived the explosion and came back? What if he's been in some hospital somewhere and just got out? What if he lost his memory and only just remembered who he is?

There has to be a logical explanation for all this and the most obvious explanation is that Hunter really is dead and this guy just looks like him—exactly like him. They might be twins except that Hunter didn't have a twin. He had one sister and she's alive and well raising three children in Wichita.

I get so wound up thinking about the past that I drive straight past my office. I have to drive around the block and concentrate hard to park in the right place. I go inside still hyperventilating about this. Now I just have to get through the rest of the day without losing my marbles.

I sit down at my desk and try to focus on work, but it doesn't get easier as the day wears on. I really hope Hunter isn't alive. That would be my worst nightmare. If he's alive, he doesn't know about Dylan.

How would it work if he came back to town and found out that I had a son by donor sperm? It would complicate things a thousand times more than they already are. My life is perfect the way it is. I don't need my dead husband coming back into my life now of all times.

Now I just have to deal with living in the same town where Hunter's double is walking around and showing up on street corners. How am I supposed to cope with that?

Chapter 2: Noah

I lean against my truck and look up from my phone when I hear a car pull into the driveway. I put my phone in my pocket as the real estate agent angles in and parks next to my truck.

I grin when she gets out of her car and I see that it's the same woman I spotted in town yesterday. She's stunning in a simple brown dress that hugs her supple curves and shows off every single goddamn inch of juicy real estate.

Natural highlights of brown, strawberry, copper, and a few white-blonde tints flash in her wild curls. They bounce every time she takes a step and her high heels accentuate her hips to make them look wider and more inviting.

She's a mother. I saw her dropping off her son at daycare, so that explains her figure, but she obviously takes care of herself. She looks just toned enough to be appealing while keeping plenty of her feminine hourglass shape. Her waist is delightfully small compared to her full chest and wide hips.

I would love to get my hands on her, but she doesn't grin back at me. She scowls and her dark brown eyes flash with something like hatred. She stands by her car and glares at me before she slams the door extra hard and stalks over to me. "Good morning," she clips in a short, annoyed voice.

"Good morning." I stick out my hand to her. She might be the most bad-tempered real estate agent ever, but I can still be civil. "I'm Noah Goldsmith."

Her shoulders slump and she lets out a long, shaky sigh. She presses her hand to her forehead and turns to one side so she doesn't look at me. She completely ignores my hand so I let it drop.

Okay. This is not how I expected this real estate viewing to go, but whatever. I'm here to buy a house, not to flirt with her.

"How long has this place been on the market?" I ask.

She turns around and faces me. Her expression relaxes, but she doesn't look any happier about this. "I'm really sorry." She sticks out her hand. "It's very nice to meet you, Mr. Goldsmith. I'm really sorry for the way I reacted to you just now. I'm Caroline Hirsch."

I don't raise my hand a second time and she pounces on me, grabs my hand, and shakes it for me. Then she waves at the house behind me and starts talking without looking at me again.

"The house has been on the market for over a year and the owners have already moved out of state, which is why the price is so low. They're anxious to move it on as soon as possible, so they would be open to negotiating the price even lower if you're interested. I have to warn you, though. The house has some damage to the interior. The previous owner had dogs and he would go to town and leave his dogs locked up inside. The carpet is....well, saying that the carpet is damaged doesn't even cover it. It's beyond ruined. The house smells terrible and most of the wallpaper and curtains are so saturated with....." She falters, gulps, and then blurts it out. "The carpet, the wallpaper, and the curtains are saturated with the stench of urine and feces. It's really disgusting. I just want to warn you ahead of time."

"Okay," I reply. "Thank you for the warning. Is the house structurally sound other than that?"

"Absolutely." She grabs a nylon zippered folder that she carries under one arm and starts unzipping it in front of me. She tries to balance it in her hands while she talks way too fast. "The previous owner got an engineer's report on the house...."

"Put it here." I take her elbow and guide her over to the truck so she can put the folder down on the hood.

She jolts at my touch like I shot her with a powerful electric shock. She recoils from me, drops the folder, and the papers in it scatter all over the ground.

We both bend down to pick them up, but when she sees me getting near her, she springs back to put distance between us. I don't understand why she's acting like this, but at least she isn't as overtly hostile as she was when she first showed up.

She stands three feet away from me pressing her hand to heart and gaping at me while I pick up her papers, tap them into a stack, and put them on the truck hood.

I wave her toward me. "Come on. I don't bite. Just show me the engineer's report."

She takes a deep, shaky breath, shivers, and finally manages to walk over to me. She gulps visibly before she starts fumbling with the papers. This meeting is obviously making her over-the-top nervous. I just can't figure out why.

She finally locates the engineer's report and hands it to me without looking at me. "You can see that the house is structurally sound. It's only twenty years old and the owner maintained it....except for the dog issue."

"That's okay. I like fixing a place up myself and I'm more interested in the land than the house."

Her head snaps around and she stares at me like I just suddenly started speaking the same language as she is. She gapes at me in shock and then jolts again. "Oh! Right! Well, as the real estate listing states, there are six ten-acre pastures, each one fenced and with a supply of water from the spring up on the hill over there." She points to a hill towering over the house and the barn nearby. "The water supply has never failed since this area was colonized back in the 1800s."

"Do you mind if I take a look around?" I ask.

"Of course. Go right ahead. Let me know if you have any questions. Just...." She blushes and catches my eye for a split second. "You'll have to excuse me if I don't go into the house with you. I've already been in there once and I don't want to do it again."

"I understand. I'll take a look and come back out and we can talk about it."

She nods and rummages in her purse. "I have the keys here somewhere...."

She locates them and holds them out to me by the keychain so she's extra sure not to touch my hand when she hands me the keys.

I go over to the house. It's a nice house on the outside. It's a standard two-story farmhouse with white-painted siding and a corrugated steel roof. Windows look out from all sides and a huge porch surrounds the front entrance. It's the perfect place to relax and look out at the rest of the sixty-acre property.

I catch a whiff of the smell even before I approach the front door. A powerful stench of toilet and unwashed dog drifts through the walls and makes me want to gag even before I get the door unlocked.

A tidal wave of stink nearly knocks me over when I open the door. I glimpse the long front hall with the living room off to one side and the open kitchen door in the back. I have to retreat to the lawn and take a few deep breaths because I work up the courage to go inside.

I pull my jacket lapel over my nose and mouth, but that doesn't help at all. The place is a cesspit of foul disgusting stench.

The living room is the worst with the downstairs parlor not much better. The kitchen isn't too bad. It doesn't have carpet or curtains or wallpaper. It's a big ranch-style kitchen with a giant wooden table, marble countertops, and a deep porcelain sink. Huge windows look out over the backyard leading to the barn.

The upstairs isn't too bad, either, except that the carpet, wallpaper, and curtains are all way too old. The windows are filthy and the whole house has a very abandoned feel, but other than that, it feels comfortable, solid, and homey.

I make it back outside and lock the front door. Caroline actually smiles at me when I rejoin her by the truck. "You didn't pass out," she observes. "I was waiting to call the rescue squad."

"It's actually a nice house. It just needs some TLC."

"It definitely does." She's been organizing her papers while I've been inside and she hands me one. "I have an extra copy of the engineer's report so you can have that one."

I take it, fold it up, and tuck it into my shirt pocket. "I want to walk out there and see the pastures. Why don't you come with me and you can explain a few things to me on the way?"

She blinks at me like she needs to think about what I just said. Then she jumps again. "Oh! Okay. I can do that. I just need to change into some more appropriate shoes. Just give me a second......"

She goes over to her car and pops the hatchback. She takes out a pair of socks and sneakers, sits down on the rear bumper, kicks off her heels, and puts on her sneakers. She tosses her heels in the back of the car and comes over to me.

She smiles again and blushes. "Don't tell anyone. I have to go in disguise when I work in the corporate world."

I glance down at her sneakers. "Do you carry those around all the time or just when you're showing a property in the country?"

"All the time. I never wear heels unless I'm showing something. I hate them." She waves toward the pastures. "Shall we go?"

I nod and shoot her a sidelong glance while we stroll down the fence line toward the other end of the property. I don't get her at all. She started out acting like she didn't want to come near me. Now she's warming up like she's a country girl underneath that slick exterior.

"The water line runs down that slope there." She points across the property toward the fence on the other side. "It splits from there and runs along that center stretch of fence with side lines going to each ten-acre section."

"Who owns those cattle there?" I ask and point to a bunch of steers in two of the fenced pastures.

"Rick Tennyson owns them. He leases the land to run his stock, but he knows the place is on the market. He's prepared to move them off if you want him to or he's very happy to continue leasing if you just want to live in the house....but you said you were interested in the land, so I guess that isn't an option."

"Who is he? Where does he live?"

"He has his own ranch right over there across the creek." She points to a line of cottonwoods along the property's bottom edge. "He's the salt of the Earth. You never met a more down-to-earth guy."

"Does he ranch over there?"

"Yeah. He has about three hundred head of cattle so he just uses this for additional grazing."

She passes her hand across her forehead again, but it's more of a cooling-down movement. She doesn't act so agitated now.

I reach one of the fences and climb over into the pasture. The steers turn around and stare at me as I squat down and start digging a hole in the sod with my fingertips.

Caroline stays where she is and watches me from the other side of the fence. She can't climb over wearing that dress. Would she if she was wearing jeans and a t-shirt? I'll probably never know.

I dig down eight inches and find deep, rich topsoil with plenty of worms. This land has been under a regular grazing routine for a long time and the soil shows it.

I squeeze a handful and it compresses nicely into a dark brown lump. I throw it back, kick the dirt back into the hole, and dust off my hands on my pants. The steers blink at me while I survey the land. It's nice land and it's all set up for what I want.

I go back over to the fence and Caroline smiles at me when I climb over it. I brush off my hands one more time. Maybe I shouldn't be showing how much of a hayseed I am, but she doesn't seem to mind. She actually looks delighted. "Did you find what you're looking for?"

"Yeah, I did." We start heading back up to the house.

"Like I said, the owner is very negotiable. He would be very reasonable about any offer, even one you might not think was high enough."

"Why do you keep telling me that?" I ask. "Shouldn't you be angling to get him the best price?"

"He doesn't care about the price. He just wants to get the property off his hands. He's the one who instructed me to tell interested buyers that he would negotiate the price down if you wanted him to."

I shake my head. "That isn't what I'm used to hearing from real estate agents."

"Have you been looking long?" she asks.

"Not long. I just came to town so this is the first property I've looked at. I already own four ranches in Texas. My brother is running them for me while I branch out and build another setup here."

She listens without looking away. She doesn't avoid me anymore.

"What about you?" I ask. "What is a single mother like you doing hiding undercover in the real estate world?"

She blushes again and looks away. "I'm just trying to make a living and keep a roof over my head and put food in my son's mouth."

"He's a cute kid. What is he—about two and a half?"

"Yeah." She beams at me and then opens her mouth like she wants to say something else, but she stops herself.

"What?" I ask.

"You really gave me a scare yesterday. I'm really sorry for acting weird when you pulled up here. I thought you were someone else."

"Who?" I ask.

"My husband—my late husband. He died five years ago while he was deployed in the Philippines and you look exactly like him. You scared the crap out of me when I saw you in town yesterday."

So that explains it. "I'm sorry to hear that. I didn't mean to scare you."

"That's okay. I can see now that you're a different person. He wasn't interested in.... all this." She waves at the property.

"What do you mean he wasn't interested in it?"

"He was an engineer. He was a city boy. He never would have checked the soil like you did. He never would have been interested in this property and he never, NEVER would have had anything to do with that house."

I have to laugh. "That's his loss and my gain."

"Anyway, I'm sorry about earlier. You really threw me for a loop yesterday. I kept imagining that he came back from the dead or that he'd been in an amnesia ward for five years or....well, my brain went into a tailspin coming up with all kinds of crazy possibilities. You have no idea how relieved I am that you aren't him."

I raise my eyebrows. "Why are you relieved? Was he an asshole or something?"

"No, not at all! It's just.....I had my son after he died. I used donor sperm and....if my husband came back....it would just be complicated. I loved him, but I had to move on after he died. Him coming back would....well, I don't know how I would handle it."

"I see." I don't know what to say so I gaze out over the property. That is an amazing story and I get a secret thrill that she isn't married or attached to anyone....except for her son.

We get back to my truck. "Do you need to see anything else or ask me anything else?" she asks.

"That's it. I've seen enough."

"Okay." She grabs her folder from the hood. "You can call the office if you want to discuss anything else."

"Can I make an appointment now to finalize the paperwork?"

"What paperwork?"

"I want to make an offer. Your owner is asking three hundred and fifty thousand. Tell him I'll give him three-twenty-five."

Her jaw drops. "You can't be serious."

"Why not? This is a nice place and it definitely won't cost me more than twenty-five thousand to replace the carpet, re-wallpaper the interior, and change the curtains."

"You're serious!" she gasps. "You could get it for so much less."

"I don't want it for less. I want to pay what it's worth and it's definitely worth three-fifty."

She shuts her mouth with difficulty and turns away to pick up her folder. "Okay, whatever you want. I'll call him when I get back to the office, but I can promise you he'll take your offer."

"Great. So can we make an appointment to finalize the paperwork?"

"Yeah. Sure." She fishes around in her purse and pulls out her phone. "When would you like to do it?"

"How about Friday? Could you get it done by then?"

She hesitates for a split second. I can't tell if it's because Friday is too soon or not soon enough. "Okay. We can do that. Just tell me what time."

"How about ten in the morning?"

She taps her phone. "Done." She looks up and beams at me. "I'll see you then."

"Perfect. Looking forward to it." I nod down at her feet. "Aren't you going to change your shoes before you go back to the office?"

She grins and her cheeks color. "I'll keep these on until the last possible second....and I won't be wearing them on Friday, either. Just warning you."

"Damn," I tease.

She laughs, gets in her car, and waves to me before she drives off. I gaze after her thinking everything over. She really is the nicest woman I've met in a long time and I'm going to see her again in just a few days. I can't wait.

Chapter 3: Caroline

Y ou did NOT!!" Willow gasps. "You did NOT sell the old Pine Hill Farm."

"Yep." I don't even try to hold back my smirk of triumph. "I'm a rock star."

"You sure are if you sold that place. No agent has been able to sell it for over a year."

"I know. I'm going in to finalize the paperwork today at ten o'clock."

"So I was right. That guy isn't Hunter."

"No, he definitely isn't." I lean against the kitchen counter and watch Dylan whizzing his toy car up and down the ramps of the giant cityscape that he and the other kids have built out of blocks. "He couldn't be more different from Hunter. They just look identical."

"So what is he doing here?" Willow asks. "How did he wind up living in the same town as a man who looks exactly like him? It's like something out of a horror movie or something."

"He comes from Texas and he's about as cowboy as they get. He has some ranching operation with his brother and they're branching out to set up shop here, too. Don't ask me why he chose this town to do it. I guess it was pure random chance."

"You know there's no such thing as coincidence, Caroline," she tells me. "There has to be some reason why he showed up on your doorstep when you're the woman who was married to his doppelganger."

"Okay. You try to figure out the reason behind it. I gotta go to work." I kiss her on the cheek and head for the door. I learned a long time ago not to kiss Dylan goodbye once he gets engrossed in his play. It's better if he doesn't see me leave.

I drive to the office and walk in on a hornet's nest of activity and excitement. "Today's the big day, Caroline!" my boss Tim Hartley tells me. "I thought we would never get the Pine Hill Farm off our books."

"You're a miracle worker, Caroline," Janine Lambert chimes in. "What did you do? Did you blindfold him when you showed him the house?"

"Blindfolding him wouldn't cover up the smell," I reply. "He likes the house and he's handy. He plans to fix it up himself."

"He's a braver man than I am if he set foot across the threshold," Paul Ackerman remarks. "Did you show him the upstairs bedrooms? They look like they have bodies hidden under the beds."

"I didn't show him anything because I didn't go inside," I reply. "He went in by himself, and yes, he saw the upstairs."

"Maybe he has a taste for rot and stench," Janine surmises.

"Maybe he has a mental disorder and he likes living in a garbage pit like that," Tim adds.

"He doesn't have a mental disorder!" I counter. "He's actually a nice guy."

Paul snorts. "He won't be after living in that place for a few weeks. He'll turn into just as much of a hermit as the previous owner."

I don't answer and I find myself blushing in spite of myself. I shouldn't get this interested in a client, but I can't help it. Noah is everything Hunter used to be and everything Hunter wasn't.

Hunter didn't understand why I liked the outdoors. He liked wining and dining in town. He never wanted to move out to the country and he sure as Holy Hell would never want to ranch cattle at a place like Pine Hill Farm.

Noah actually seemed to like it when I put on my sneakers and hiked out to the pasture fence with him. I enjoyed that....but I'm not thinking about him that way. He's a client and he's coming in to finalize a sale. That's all.

I get busy organizing all the papers he has to sign and initial, but if he already owns property in Texas, he's probably used to the routine.

I find my heart racing as ten o'clock approaches. I wish now that I didn't freak out so much when I met him at the property. I wish now that I dealt with it better, but the viewing certainly ended well.

Maybe I can pull my head out of the clouds long enough to handle this meeting the right way. I definitely have some damage control to do where my customer service skills are concerned. I made the sale, but not because I charmed him with my professionalism and social dexterity.

I fidget and squirm as I count down the minutes until ten o'clock. I get up from my desk when I hear the doorbell chime at five minutes before the hour.

I leave my office, but when I get to reception to greet Noah, I find Paul, Janine, and Tim already there. Tim strides up to Noah and extends his hand. "I have to be the first person to shake the hand of the man who bought the Pine Hill Farm. We thought that place would never sell. We owe you a big one for this, man."

Noah chuckles and shakes his hand. "I'm glad I could take it off your hands."

Paul and Janine crowd around gushing about how bad the property is and how Noah's sanity will crack if he lives there for too long.

He smiles and laughs at their jokes. He takes all their comments in good grace and I can't help but remark on how similar he looks to Hunter.

Noah looks amazing in a pair of fitted canvas cargo pants with tons of pockets, black leather boots, and a black leather vest over a crisp blue business shirt. He carries a zippered case under one arm, but this one is black leather instead of nylon.

He looks like the Texan version of a very successful businessman who is rich enough and confident enough that he no longer has to wear a suit. He acts perfectly casual and at ease with the idea of buying a piece of property.

The other three agents finally get tired of making a big deal about him and they part ways to let me through when I come forward.

I can't stop myself from blushing when I smile up at him. "Good morning. Sorry about all this. We've had an office competition to see who could sell the Pine Hill Farm."

"That's okay. Let's get it taken care of so you can take home your prize."

I have to laugh. "There's no prize—just bragging rights."

"And you already got that, Caroline," Tim chimes in from behind me.

"You deserve it," Noah tells me. "You definitely sold the house."

"By telling you what a dump it is? Hardly."

"No, by telling me that it was sound except for the soft furnishings ....and you sold me on all the other features—the water, the neighbors, the infrastructure. You knocked it out of the park."

I shuffle my feet when I see the look in his eyes. I know that look too well. I've seen Hunter looking at me like that too many times.

I shouldn't assume Noah's facial expressions mean the same thing that Hunter's did. Noah is a completely different person, but I can't help but get a stomach full of butterflies when Noah looks deeply into my eyes in a way that means he's thinking about something more—or it would mean that if Hunter was looking at me like that.

I wave toward my office. "Follow me and I'll show you where to go."

He follows me into my office and takes a seat by my desk. I have to sit next to him so I can show him the sales agreement.

I flip through each page showing him where to sign and initial and then, when he finishes, I give his signature a notary seal.

I finally put the last dates and initials on the agreement and sit back in my own desk chair. "There you go! It's all done." I take the keys out of my drawer and hand them to him. "Good luck with it. I hope your ranching operation works out."

"It will." He puts the keys in his case and turns to me. "Now that we aren't client and agent anymore, how would like to go out with me tomorrow night?"

I freeze and stare at him with my mouth open. Did he really just ask me out?

He waves his hand in front of my eyes. "Hello? Did you hear me?"

"Yes! I heard you." I shake myself. "Sorry. I'm flattered, but I don't think it's a good idea."

"Why not? Going out with me won't cause any conflict with the property sale. It's all finished."

"It isn't that. I was just thinking....I don't think it's a good idea to bring a stepfather into my son's life."

He bursts out laughing and his cheeks color. His black eyes sparkle in a way that says he's genuinely delighted with what I just said—or he would be delighted if Hunter was laughing and blushing like that.

"I wasn't offering myself as a stepfather for your son. I was asking you out on a date. I asked *you* out, not your son. Come on. What do you say? No strings attached. Just you and me and a good time."

I gasp and jolt back in my chair. "No way! How can you even suggest that?"

He blinks and then bursts into an even more delighted fit of laughter. "I didn't mean *that*!"

I can't look at him. I hold up my hands and get to my feet the way that all real estate agents use when they want to end a meeting. "Thank you for coming in. I'm pleased we could finish this sale. Let me know if I can do anything else for you again."

"You can go out with me. What do you say—no good times or anything like that." He laughs again. "Do you ever get any free time away from your son—any time when he can go somewhere else so you can get some time to yourself?"

I shrug and squirm some more. This conversation is making me extremely embarrassed. "He goes to my parents' house every other weekend. I'm driving him up there after work today."

"There you go. That's perfect. So you'll be all alone tomorrow night with nothing to do but go out with me."

I stare at him realizing in sudden horror that he's right. I have nothing planned for tomorrow night. I was just planning to stay home and listen to the silence where Dylan should be. That's what I usually do when he goes out of town to visit my parents.

Why shouldn't I go out with someone? It isn't like I don't find Noah attractive. I do, and if he isn't offering himself as a stepfather for

Dylan, why shouldn't I just go out with him to have a good time—and not in *that* way?

I definitely will NOT have a good time with him in *that* way. It's just going out on Saturday night. That's all. It's no big deal, so why am I getting serious heart palpitations from thinking about it?

He starts to turn away. "All right. I got my answer. Thank you for everything. I'll see you around."

"Wait!" I blurt out. "Okay. I'll go out with you."

He bursts into a huge grin and his eyes twinkle. "Great. You have my number. Why don't you text me with the time and your address and I'll pick you up?"

Chapter 4: Noah

I pull up in front of Caroline's house and head up to the front porch, only for her to come out before I get there. She smiles at me while she locks the door behind her. "You look nice," she tells me.

I look nicer than she's ever seen me before. I can clean up when I want to scrape the cow shit out from under my fingernails. I do own a few suits and I selected a dark grey one for tonight, but I still can't bring myself to put on a tie.

I promised myself in high school that I would never wear a tie if I could possibly avoid it. I've managed to dodge that bullet so far and I'm not about to start.

I don't look nearly as nice as she does. She wears another tight-fitting dress like the one had on when I first met her, but this one is black with large, bright, white and fuchsia flowers printed on it at strategic locations. It accents the highlights in her hair and makes her look stunning.

She's also wearing a pair of black heels that make her hips stand out exactly the way I remember. She's seriously tempting, but I have to behave myself a little longer.

"You aren't wearing your sneakers," I tell her. "What's wrong? Are you sick or something?"

She laughs and her features light up. Is she blushing? "I considered it. I really did, but they didn't quite go with the dress."

"You could have worn shorts and a t-shirt and you would look just as good."

Now I know she's blushing. "Thanks."

I open the passenger door of my truck and she climbs in still smirking at me. She grins at the truck like she's getting away with something by riding around with a cowboy like me.

I catch her grinning at me when I get behind the wheel and start driving into town. "So where are we going?" she asks.

"I told you we'd have a good time and not in *that* way, so I thought we could go to the county fair. What do you think?"

"Sounds great!" She grins even more broadly and then her features wilt. "Now I really wish I'd brought my sneakers. My feet are going to be killing me if I spend all night walking around."

"Well, maybe you won't be walking around ALL night. I still have a reputation to protect, you know."

She bursts into giggles. "I'm sure you do."

I can't help but grin back at her. This conversation is priceless. "Don't worry about your feet. I have the solution."

"What solution is that—and don't tell me you plan to carry me around all evening."

I wait until I stop at a traffic light, reach behind her seat, and pull a pair of sneakers from the back. I hand them to her. "They're mine. They might be a little big, but they'll be more comfortable than those heels."

She studies them. "Thanks. They don't have any cow shit on them."

I laugh. "I can change that if you want me to. You've been in the city too long. You need to be baptized in cow shit so the cows recognize you again."

"Good point. How's the house coming along?"

"It's coming along good. I threw out all the old carpet and curtains and the furniture in the upstairs bedrooms. I scrubbed down the floors and the new carpet is going in next week, so it's shaping up. I have to find someone to do the wallpaper and then I'll be all set."

"You said you liked doing it yourself."

"I do, but I don't have time to replace the wallpaper in a house that size. I might as well hire someone else to do it."

She gazes at the side of my face while I drive. I cast glances at her as often as I can without driving off the road. "What's up? Why are you looking at me like that?"

"I just keep trying to figure out which of your facial expressions mean the same thing that Hunter's meant. It's surreal trying to get to know someone who looks so much like him but who has such a radically different personality." She turns away and shakes her head. "Sorry. I'll try to stop talking about him."

"You don't have to. I don't mind."

"See? That on its own is surreal. Most men would feel threatened by a woman talking about her dead husband all the time."

"You don't talk about him all the time and why should I feel threatened by someone who's dead? It isn't like he can come back from the grave and fight me for you. Besides, it's normal that it would be weird for you to hang out with me when I look exactly like someone you had such a close relationship with."

"I'm glad you understand," she murmurs under her breath. "You're a lot more okay with it than I am."

"Of course I'm okay with it. You're going out with me, not him."

"I would be going out with him if he was here."

"But he isn't here."

She turns and looks directly at the side of my face. "Doesn't it bother you that I might be going out with you because you look like my dead husband?"

"*Are* you going out with me because I look like your dead husband? Is that the reason you agreed to go out with me? You told me that first day at the farm that you got scared when you saw me in town. You said it bothered you that I look like him and then, at your office, you made it sound like me looking like him would put you off from going out with me. None of that sounds like you're going out with me because of that."

She turns back to the window. "You're right."

"Does it bother you?" I ask.

"Kind of. Okay, it bothers me a lot."

"Why?"

"Because I...." She trails off, and just then, I pull into the parking lot at the fairgrounds.

I switch off the engine, and when I look over at her, she glances up into my eyes.

I nod down at her lap. "Put your sneakers on and let's go have some fun."

She bursts into a grin and kicks off her heels. She puts on my sneakers and ties them. "Oh, my God! My feet are swimming in these things."

"You can audition to play Bozo the Clown." I get out of the car and open her door for her.

I have to stop myself from taking her hand. I really want to hold her hand and make this a real date, but I can wait.

She grins at me and then flaps her feet in a very clownish way. She makes me laugh, and without thinking, I take her hand.

She blushes, but she doesn't take her hand away. I buy our tickets and we start walking through the fair. "What do you want to do first?" I ask. "Do you want to ride the Tilt-o'-Whirl?"

"Let's leave that until last, eat a couple of hotdogs and milkshakes before we leave, and then go on the Tilt-O'-Whirl so I can puke all over the floor of your truck."

"Ooookkkkkkaaaayyyy....scratch that," I tell her. "What do you want to do?"

"We could go on the Ferris Wheel. That's relatively harmless."

"All right. What about the bumper cars? Do you like that or will that make you puke, too?"

"It won't make me puke, but I can be ruthless. I'm just warning you ahead of time."

"Oh, now you're throwing down the gauntlet. We'll see who can be the most ruthless."

We get into the line for the Ferris wheel and she keeps grinning at me on the way to the front. We get into the seat and the wheel carries us upward. We stop at the three-quarter mark to wait while another car loads beneath us.

"Why did you ask me out?" she asks suddenly. "Most guys don't want to have anything to do with a single mother."

"Why not?" I ask. "Why should that make any difference?"

"It just does. Most guys don't want to spend their lives raising a child that isn't theirs."

"Well, I'm not most guys."

She turns to beam up at me. "I know you aren't."

"As far as I'm concerned, you being a single mother is just evidence that you would be a perfect mother to *my* children. It's proof that you know how to do the job because you're already doing it. You're already responsible and caring and attentive and engaged with your child. What could be more attractive than that?"

She turns bright red and looks away. She doesn't answer. Which part of that made her uncomfortable—that I mentioned her being a mother to my children?

I take a chance, take hold of her chin, and turn her around to face me. She looks so fucking beautiful in the fair lights that I have to kiss her.

Her lips feel incredibly soft and delightful and I ease in. She starts to kiss me back, but at that moment, the Ferris wheel jolts and starts moving. She screams when it swoops over the top and starts to descend.

I laugh when I hear her scream, and just because, I put my arm around her shoulders and pull her close. She eases into me and my stomach flips. It's working. We're on a real date and I just kissed her for the first time.

She doesn't try to pull away as the wheel keeps rotating around and around. She screams a second time when the wheel reaches the top and starts falling again. She scoots just a little closer to me until her majestic body is glued right up against me. She quivers all over with fear and excitement. I want to touch her more, but this isn't the moment.

The wheel stops at the one-quarter mark to let people get out and we're stranded thirty feet off the ground. She glances up at me and we're sitting so close together with my arm around her that I have to kiss her again.

I tighten my arm around her shoulders and pull her right against my chest. She melts into my lips and her sweet breath lights me on fire. She's beyond perfect and she's right here kissing me.

I barely have to do anything to nudge her mouth open and then our tongues are swirling and dancing and exploring each other in incredible ways. I can't get enough of this.

I slide my fingers into her hair, but at that moment, the wheel falls the rest of the way and the carnies open the gate to let us out.

I take her hand as soon as we get onto the ground. "Do you want to eat something or get a milkshake now?" I ask.

"Sure. What are you hungry for?"

I'm hungry for her, but I don't say that. I lead her toward the food stalls. "We could get burgers.... or that place has Indian food."

"Let's go with burgers."

We get our food and sit down on a bench looking out at the fair. "Why did you choose to move here of all places?" she asked. "Why did you leave Texas?"

I shrug. I didn't think the conversation would turn to this so soon, but she's already told me chapter and verse about her dead husband. Why shouldn't I be honest?

"I had a girlfriend. We split up about a year ago and I decided to leave town....just so I could start over somewhere else where no one knew me. My brother and I were already planning to expand into another area so I did some research and chose to move here."

"Why did you break up?"

She asks it so straightforwardly. She doesn't betray any embarrassment that I had a girlfriend before. Why should she?

"She didn't want to get serious," I tell her. "She just wanted to play around and keep everything in the present and never think about or plan any kind of future between us. She thought everything was great the way it was and she didn't see any reason to change it. After a while, it got to the point where I had to start planning a future with someone.

If it wasn't going to be with her, then I had to cut the cord and go plan it with someone else."

She blushes again, but she doesn't act like I said anything strange or out of this world. "That's understandable."

"Is it? She made it out that there was something wrong with wanting to plan a future and settle down with someone. She thought everyone should be happy to just cruise along and be happy with today."

"It's kind of the same thing that I did when I got pregnant with Dylan," she replies. "I had to start looking toward the future and I was still too emotional about Hunter to think about dating another guy. If I wasn't going to really go out of my way to put myself on the market and find another husband, I just had to take a dive and get pregnant. I couldn't keep living in the past."

"Yeah, I can totally understand that. I think it's admirable that you got pregnant on your own."

She spins around and her eyes widen staring at me. "You do?"

"Sure. I donated sperm when I was a starving, struggling college student. It would be pretty hypocritical of me to do that and then judge the people who use it to get pregnant, wouldn't it?"

She studies me with another intense stare. "You really aren't like other guys, you know that?"

I laugh nervously. "Don't tell anyone or you'll blow my disguise. Everything depends on blending in with the crowd."

"Your secret is safe with me as long as you keep my secret about being a closet country girl."

"You can be a country girl with me anytime."

I find myself beaming at her. I would love to kiss her again right now, but maybe what we did on the Ferris wheel was just a fluke.

Without warning, she slides down the bench and squeezes right up against my body. She sighs and rests her head on my shoulder while she sips her milkshake.

That feeling floods me with happiness. This is so good—so sweet and easy and perfect. I don't want to go anywhere or do anything or see anything. I just want to sit here and savor the feeling of her cuddling up to me.

I finish my burger, and since I have my right hand free, I rest it on her knee. She doesn't pull away or protest. This is so, so good.

Chapter 5: Noah

Caroline finishes her milkshake and we throw all our burger wrappers and cups in the trash. "Let's go do some damage on the bumper cars," I tell her.

We hold hands on our way there and while we're standing in line. She grins at me while we strap into the cars, and as soon as the whistle blows, she rockets away and starts whizzing around the track.

I race to keep up with her, but she gets the jump on me, comes barreling around the corner, and T-bones my car at top speed. She giggles when I curse under my breath, reverses away, and takes off like a bat out of hell.

I gun it trying to catch up with her, but she makes another circuit and comes at me for another collision. I see her coming, pull my foot off the gas at the last second, and she goes hurtling past me.

Now I'm on her tail and I smash her into the guard rail. She lurches hard against her safety straps and I crow in triumph. "Ha! Take that!"

"I'm gonna get you for that!" she yells back, but she's still laughing and grinning like a fool as I reverse away and we go back out onto the track.

We trade shots and laugh at each other for the full five minutes until our cars stop. Caroline blushes and laughs as we leave the track, take each other's hands, and head down the causeway toward the rides.

"Remind me never to drive anywhere with you," I tell her once we both calm down.

"Hey, you were giving as good as you got out there. Don't pretend you weren't."

"I can be reasonable when I need to be."

She laughs and squeezes my hand. "I'm actually a really conservative driver, but I have to take out my murderous aggressions somewhere. I save it for the bumper cars."

"You better." I hook my arm around her shoulder and kiss the side of her head. I want to do more, but we're in public here.

We go on a few more rides, play a few games, eat ice cream, and generally waste a bunch of time screwing around being stupid, but she seems to be enjoying herself. She never stops me from kissing her, holding her hand, or putting my arm around her.

I finally steer her toward the parking lot. It's time to go home. "I had a good time tonight," she tells me, "and not in *that* way."

"Me, too. We should do it again another time."

"If you want to."

I glance over at her. "Really? You would go out with me again?"

"Sure. Just tell me ahead of time if I should wear sneakers or heels."

I pull her to a stop in front of my truck. "I meant what I said. You could wear sneakers all the time and you would still look like a million bucks."

She blushes. "I have to blend in with the crowd, too."

The lights from the fair catch her eyes again and I don't give myself a second to hesitate. I kiss her again, and this time, we're far enough away from everything that I don't have to pull away. No one will interrupt us here.

I thread my fingers into her hair and pull her into my kiss. Her mouth relaxes open and our tongues join in that sultry, steamy dance of succulent rapture. She tenses when I press her lower back into me. I want her, but I don't want to rush anything.

Her hands fly to my arms in a very soft pushing motion. That tiny suggestion of resistance makes me ache for her and I lace my fingers into her other hand to steer her arms around my neck.

She obliges, and once she has her arms in that position, she sinks into my arms so magically that I have to kiss her harder. I grab a handful of her beautiful, round ass and crush her against me.

She gasps and her breathing shortens when she feels how hard I am. I want to take her right now, but that can wait. She shivers and her pelvis winds up corkscrewing on my bulging knob.

I tighten my hand into a fist in her hair and kiss her for all I'm worth. She makes me so hot, but she's also beyond beautiful in a comfortable appealing way. I want to attack her, but at the same time, I want to treat her gently and protect her from any harm.

She doesn't stop kissing me. She matches my energy exactly and escalates with me. Is it possible she wants this as much as I do?

I let go of her hair, caress down her back, and scoop both hands up to her magnificent breasts. She whimpers in my mouth when I massage them through her dress. Her body trembles and she winds her hips to grind on my hardness. Holy shit, she's on fire!

I lean forward and wind up taking a step. She bumps into the truck and then I'm on top of her. I smash her under my weight driving my junk between her legs, but her dress won't let her spread them for me.

That's just as well, because if she did, I would probably tear her clothes off right here. She moans and undulates under me matching my rhythm. Her plaintive noises rise to a tempest in my ears and drive me crazy.

I flex my legs working into her and I grab the cargo rack above her head to give myself leverage for my thrusts. She keeps whining and sobbing like I really am taking her right now. I wish I was.

Her arms stay wrapped around my neck and her mouth fills my brain with all kinds of luscious fantasies about tasting her and feeling her mouth teasing me to new heights. I can think of so many things I want to do with her.

I want to turn her around and bend her over the seat. I want to climb into the cab and get her to straddle me right here in the parking lot.

I haul myself off her with a massive effort. Her eyes drive me insane when she looks up at me all delirious with pleasure and desire. She really wants it, but I am definitely not making our first time in some parking lot and definitely not standing out in public where anyone can gawk at us.

I pull away and she bites her lip when I open the door for her. She climbs in without a word and I get behind the wheel. Neither of us grin at all when I start the motor and start driving across town.

She takes off my sneakers and sticks them behind the seat, but she doesn't put on her heels. She sits there in her bare feet for the rest of the drive.

I pull up to the first traffic light and glance over at her. She stares up at me with that wild, drunken look from the parking lot. She's beyond hot and those eyes tell me more than I ever wanted to know.

She reaches over and slips her hand onto my thigh—high enough to give me a hint but not high enough to actually do anything.

Without thinking, I grab her hand and slide it the rest of the way onto my knob. She can feel how throbbing hard I am and having her touch me in traffic like this makes me strain and twitch in her hand.

She starts squeezing me through my pants and I gasp once before the light turns green. I start driving, but she doesn't stop stroking me. I have to fight myself under control to stay focused on the road, but every traffic light brings that feeling crashing into my brain.

Her hand feels unimaginably good. I want to do everything with her. I want her to finish me off at the same time that I want us to just be getting started.

I park in front of her house and turn to kiss her, but she's already leaning toward me to kiss me, too. She rises out of her chair trying to reach me and her hand between my legs feels so fucking incredible that I need to do something.

I lunge out of my seat and attack her mouth hard enough to drive her back into place. I maul her breasts, and when she gives a small shriek of pleasure, I swivel onto my knees in front of her.

I start pushing up her dress and her eyes glaze over with ravenous madness watching me pull down her panties. Her milky white thighs spread when I push her knees apart and I dive between her legs.

She sobs and cries on my mouth as I settle in for the long haul. She tries to lean back in the chair, but she has to sit upright. I reach under the seat and pull the lever to make her lie back and she screams as my mouth closes over her swollen, dripping tissues.

She arches her back pushing into my face and she writhes as her delicious cries escalate to screams. I grab one of her breasts and slide two fingers inside her. Her flesh spasms and twitches with rising desire as she nears her climax. I love watching her contort on my mouth and her juices give me superhuman power.

I drive into her feeling her honey flooding onto my hand. She hooks her heels on my shoulders and bucks into me screaming like anything. Holy fuck, she's insane!

She finally jolts back shrieking for the whole neighborhood to hear and I drill her hard with my hand. My package hurts from throbbing so hard. Everything about her makes me ravenous for her.

She collapses whimpering and panting on the seat. I lick her very softly and gently reveling in the blissful little twitches running through her body and the sad, whining sobs she gives every time I hit a sensitive spot. I could stay down here all night.

She drags herself off the seat, sits up, and when I start kissing her again, she runs her hand between my legs and starts stroking me again. "Please......" she croaks between kisses. "Please....I need you......I need you....now....."

She tries to pull me toward her, and when I don't do anything, she stuffs her hot little hand down my pants and into my shorts.

Mind-blowing heat seizes me when her bare fingers close around my shaft. She leaves me no peace when she starts stroking me harder and faster and moaning, "Please....I need you......"

She wants me to take her right now in the truck. I could so easily, but that isn't what I want, either. I could take her inside and spend all night filling her with pleasure, but instead, I straighten up and pull her hand out.

"Not yet, baby," I whisper. "Not like this."

"Please...." She kisses me again. "I need you so bad!"

She whines these words in a cracked undertone. Her voice twists my insides. Fuck, I want her so bad, but something stops me.

"Soon, baby," I tell her between kisses. "Soon."

"Now!" she sobs. "I need you now."

I can't stop kissing her when she whimpers like that. I need her now, too, but waiting will make it so much better.

I sit back on my heels and she doesn't stop me from sliding up her panties and pulling down her dress. She gulps and her face spasms with agony, but she doesn't argue.

I go back to my own seat and I have to think hard before I make up my mind what I'm going to do. I want her. I want her all fucking night, but there are other things I want more.

I'm just about to get out of the truck to open her door for her when her phone trills. She jumps on her handbag, pulls out her phone, and groans when she sees the screen. "Oh, great!"

"What's wrong?" I ask. "Is it another cowboy moving to town who wants to buy a ranch?"

"It's Hunter's parents. They want to get together with me and Dylan next weekend."

"Their son has been dead for five years," I point out. "Why do they still want to get together with you?"

"I know it's weird, but they want to stay in my life for some reason. They don't get that Dylan isn't Hunter's child. I guess they want to think of him as that. They want him to be their grandson."

"I guess there's nothing wrong with that as long as they treat you both well."

She snorts. "It just makes it that much more complicated for me to move on. I wouldn't want them to find out if I ever decided to bring another man into Dylan's life."

"Have you ever asked them?"

"I don't dare. I never know how to handle them."

"Would you like me to handle them for you?" I ask. "You could invite me to the meeting as your date."

She makes a face and stuffs her phone back into her handbag. "They would definitely NOT appreciate me going out with someone who looks so much like Hunter."

"Why wouldn't they appreciate it? It has nothing to do with them and you said I'm totally different from him."

"You are. I just don't want to deal with whatever their reactions would be. I just wish they'd move on the way I have."

"Well, if you need me to straighten them out, you let me know."

She laughs and shuts her handbag. "You'll be the first person I call."

That's my cue. I get out, open her door for her, and she steps out of the truck in her bare feet. She carries her heels in her hand and follows me when I lead her up to the porch.

I kiss her on the porch for a while. "Can I call you about going out again sometime?" I ask her.

"I'd like that," she murmurs. "I had a really good time tonight......in *that* way."

Now it's my turn to laugh. "Get inside and behave yourself."

"Thanks." She kisses me. "Bye."

She unlocks the door and slips inside. I head back to my truck feeling.... hopeful. This is going so much better than I ever thought it could. If it keeps going this way, there's no limit to where it could end up.

Chapter 6:
Caroline

"**M**ommy—look at me!" Dylan jumps up and down on top of the jungle gym until I smile and wave at him. Then he goes over to the slide, sits down, and pushes off.

I meet him at the bottom and give him a hug. "Congratulations, buddy! You can go down the slide all by yourself now, can't you?"

He takes off to the other side of the playground, but when it comes time to climb up on a bigger jungle gym, he spots some other kids above him. They must be about seven or eight and they can do a whole lot more than he can.

He watches them for a minute and then runs back to the little kid's jungle gym. Some much smaller babies crawl around on its lowest deck which is only about three feet off the ground.

He looks so much bigger than they do. It's hard to remember him ever being that small or to imagine him ever getting as big as the older kids even though I know he will get that big someday.

The older kids' parents sit on the benches talking and don't even watch their kids play anymore. Some of them even wander off to the bathrooms or the café nearby.

They act so casual about their children's safety, but their kids can obviously handle themselves. They move effortlessly from one obstacle to another. They're never in any danger of falling, and when they do, they pick themselves up and keep going. I can't imagine Dylan ever being that independent. It seems like another world from my reality with a two-year-old who needs my constant attention.

A yell catches my ear from across the park. "Dylan—hi! Hey, Dylan!"

He doesn't hear and I turn to see Claire and Ron Jamison coming toward the jungle gym. Hunter's parents don't look a day older and they go straight to the jungle gym to greet Dylan.

He lets them hug him and then he starts yelling for them to watch him go down the slide, too. They've been in his life since birth. To him, they're just as much a part of his life as my parents are.

They watch him and talk to him for a while before Claire comes over to me. She greets me with a big smile and gives me a hug. "You look fantastic! How do you do it? How do you stay so youthful and beautiful raising a two-year-old and working full time?"

I try to laugh it off. "I guess I'm just blessed with good genes. How are you and Ron doing?"

"We're great. Charlene came down to visit last weekend." That's Hunter's sister, the mother of the Jamisons' real grandchildren. "They want to go to Disneyland and they want us to go with them."

"That's great," I reply.

"We'd like to take Dylan if you're okay with it. I know he's a little young for that....."

I grimace and try to keep my tone diplomatic. "I think he's a little too young to go traveling across the country and I doubt he would even appreciate Disneyland at his age. Maybe wait until he gets older."

"Okay. You're the boss." She squeezes my arm and I try to end the conversation by watching Dylan. He's finally worked up the courage to go to the bigger jungle gym, now that the older kids have moved on to somewhere else.

Ron encourages him to climb higher and stands close enough that he'll be able to catch Dylan if he falls. I should be grateful to the Jamisons for trying to stay involved in Dylan's life. I should be glad I have two sets of grandparents helping out instead of just one.

It's kind of hard not to resent them for interfering, though. Dylan isn't their grandchild and their presence and constant contact makes it even harder for me to put Hunter into my past.

I could never tell them that, though. They stay involved with me and Dylan to keep Hunter alive which is exactly what I don't want to do. I don't want to hurt them, but sometimes I wonder if them hanging around is hurting me instead.

Dylan gets to the top of a much higher slide and balks. He won't slide down, and when he returns to the ladder, he can't bring himself to climb down that, either.

Ron holds out his hands to the little boy and Dylan finally lets Ron lift him down to the ground. Dylan takes off back toward the little kid's jungle gym and Ron comes toward me and Claire.

All at once, Claire screams out loud and her hand flies to her heart. "Oh, my God! Sweet Jesus!"

"What?" I spin around to find her hyperventilating and shaking like a leaf.

"Over there....! Oh, my God!" She points a trembling finger across the park and her voice cracks with horror. "It can't be! It can't be! Oh, my God! Merciful Jesus! Oh, my God!"

I turn around to see what she's pointing at and all the puzzle pieces click into place when I see Noah standing outside a store across town. He's looking at his phone. He has no idea that we're even here.

"It's okay." I pat Claire's arm. "It isn't Hunter. It's Noah Goldsmith. He just moved to town. He looks exactly like Hunter, but it isn't him."

"Oh, my God! Oh, my God!" Claire keeps panting. Her shoulders heave and she can't calm down.

"Sit down, darling." Ron takes her arm and tries to lead her toward the benches, but she's panicking so badly that she's irrational.

"It isn't Hunter, Claire," I tell her. "You don't have to worry. Hunter didn't come back from the grave."

Ron frowns across the street at Noah who leans on his truck while he taps on his phone. He's totally oblivious to the effect he's having on these unsuspecting old people.

"Are you sure it isn't him?" Ron asks. "He's an exact copy of Hunter. Maybe he.... I don't know. Maybe he lost his memory or something."

"I freaked out and thought the same thing when I first saw Noah, too, but he couldn't be more different. Look. I'll introduce you and then you'll understand."

I race across the park and dash across the street. Noah looks up and bursts into a grin when he sees me coming toward him. "Hello," he exclaims.

"Hi. Do you see those two old people over there in the park? They're Hunter's parents and his mother is freaking out because she just saw you over here. Would you mind coming over and letting me introduce you so they can understand that you aren't their dead son come back from the grave?"

He laughs and shoves his phone in his pocket. "Sure. I've never been mistaken for a zombie so much in my life."

I resist the urge to hold his hand on our way back to the playground, and when we get closer, I realize with a pang exactly what I'm about to do. "Just don't do or say anything....about us," I murmur under my breath.

"Okay. I won't."

Claire panics even more as Noah gets closer to her. She keeps gulping deep breaths of air, looking everywhere on all sides to avoid looking at him, and her cries of, "Oh, my God! Oh, my God!" keep getting louder. Other parents at the playground are starting to notice the commotion.

I pull Noah over to stand in front of Ron and Claire. "Noah Goldsmith, this is Ron and Claire Jamison. Noah just moved here and bought a piece of property outside of town. He's a cattle rancher. That's how we met. I was his real estate agent for the sale."

Ron recovers first, straightens up, and extends his hand. "Good to meet you, son. Please excuse my wife's reaction. For a second there, it really looked like our son was coming back from the dead."

"I understand, Sir," Noah replies. "Caroline explained the whole situation to me."

"So.... you're a cattle rancher?" Ron continues.

"That's right. My brother and I own four properties outside Lubbock, Texas, and I just moved here to do the same thing. Caroline tells me that your son was an engineer and wasn't interested in anything outdoors."

"Yeah." Ron rubs his chin and frowns. "That's right."

Noah turns to Claire. "It's a pleasure to meet you, Ma'am." He extends his hand to her and she springs away with a petrified shriek.

Ron and I both move over to her on either side. "It's okay, Claire," I tell her. "He won't hurt you."

"I'm sorry to hear about your son, Ma'am," Noah tells her. "I hear he died on deployment overseas."

Claire stares at him like he's speaking Chinese. Then she bursts into tears and takes off running through the park. Her loud sobs drift to my ears as she recedes into the distance.

Ron gives me a pained look, mumbles, "I better go after her," and he leaves, too. He strides away on Claire's track, and in a minute, they both pass out of sight.

"Well, that's never happened to me before," Noah remarks.

"Sorry about that. Thanks for coming over. I appreciate you being so nice to them."

"Don't mention it. I'm just sorry it's so hard for her. I really didn't know any of this was going to happen when I moved to this town."

"Don't worry about it," I tell him. "They don't live here, and now that they know you're here, they won't freak out as much if they see you around town—at least, I hope they won't."

"Maybe they'll avoid coming to town altogether."

I have to smile up at him. "Maybe."

Just then, Dylan calls to me from the top of the jungle gym. "Mommy—look at me!"

"I better go." Noah leans and kisses me on the cheek.

I get a wave of butterflies in my stomach that he's kissing me in public right in front of my son, but Dylan isn't even looking at us and no one around notices.

"Bye," Noah whispers and walks away.

Chapter 7: Noah

I squint into a giant dust cloud and shield my eyes as the big stock truck backs up to the fence. I swing the gate out of the way and the driver jumps down to open the truck's loading gate.

The steers leap out and take off running into their new pasture—my new pasture. The driver waits just long enough for the steers to vacate the truck before he hands me the invoice, yells, "Thanks!" and jumps back into the cab. He pulls out and the dust cloud floats away.

Now I'm all alone with my new steers. The property looks right now that they're here. It really feels like it's coming alive. The cattle trot around for a while before they settle down and start grazing.

I stand at the fence admiring them for a little longer before I go up the house to my home office. The house feels good, too, now that all the old crappy carpet, wallpaper, and curtains have been replaced. It only took me a week straight of cleaning this place. Now it feels like a home.

I sit down behind my desk, turn on my computer, and click over to my bank account to pay the invoice when I hear another car coming up the driveway. I go out front to see a courier van pull in front of the house.

The driver hands me a package and holds out his clipboard. "Sign here."

"What is it?" I ask.

"No idea." He takes back the clipboard. "Thanks. Bye."

I go inside frowning at the package. I didn't order anything. Then I see the return address. It's from Walter Evans, the lawyer handling my parents' estate.

I call him on my phone while I cut open the package with my pocket knife. "Did you send me something?" I ask.

"Oh, yeah. I forgot to tell you."

"Thanks a lot," I growl. "What is it?"

"It's title transfer paperwork from your dad's ranch properties, two from your maternal grandparents' estate.....and there are some sealed documents for you."

"What sealed documents?"

"I can't tell you that. That's why they're sealed. You just have to open them and find out. Get a real estate agent to check the title transfer paperwork and then sign and notarize all the spots I marked for you. You can courier them back to me in the envelope I provided."

"Okay. Will do."

I hang up and tear into the documents. He's right. The stack of paperwork is nearly three feet thick—okay, maybe not that thick, but there's plenty of it. I need a real estate agent and I just so happen to know one.

I make one last check that the steers are settling in before I get in my truck and drive to town to Caroline's office. Her boss Tim isn't around to make a fuss about my ranch so I give my name to the receptionist who calls Caroline. "Noah Goldsmith is here to see you."

Caroline comes out smiling at me. "Well, look who's here."

I wave my stack of documents at her. "I need to consult with you in a professional capacity. Sorry."

She laughs. "Come on in. That is quite a sizeable stack of paperwork."

"I know it is."

"So what is it?"

'It's a bunch of title transfer documentation from my parents' estate. They died last year and the lawyers have been going through everything transferring my parents' property to me and my brother, Tom. Some of the property was locked up in a family trust so it's only going through now."

"All right. Let me see." She sits down behind her desk, takes the stack, and starts flipping through it. "Wow. There are some pretty impressive properties here. I didn't realize your family was such a ranching empire."

"It wasn't. It was scattered all over the place, but now Tom and I are trying to bring it together."

She pauses while she reads through it. "This one seems pretty straightforward. Sign on the spots your lawyer indicated and I'll notarize them."

We work through the documents one at a time and she points out tricky spots in each one that might need more attention or legal maneuvering to fully transfer title.

I'm in the middle of signing a different document when she says, "What's this?"

I look up to find her studying a large manila envelope at the bottom of the stack. My name is on the front. "That must be the sealed documents he mentioned. Yeah. Here it is."

I turn over the envelope to find a large sticker over the flap. It has a bunch of lines of legalese, several signatures, and a notary seal.

"I might as well open it and find out what it is." I slit the sticker and pull out another pack of papers.

"What is it?" Caroline asks.

I start flipping through it and freeze when I find a letter handwritten in my mother's handwriting.

Dear Noah,

If you're reading this, it means I'm gone and now you know what a coward I am that I never had the courage to tell you the truth to your face. When I was seventeen, I met a young Navy sailor at the Port of San Diego. We went out for one night and I got pregnant with his child. I never told him, and after he left San Diego, I ran away and moved to another city where no one knew me so no one would find out that I had a child out of wedlock. I lied to everyone and told everyone that my husband was dead and that I moved out of state to start over.

I met Sam Goldsmith while I was still pregnant with you and he raised you as his own son. I got pregnant with Tom after that and no one ever found out that you boys had different fathers.

I'm so sorry I lied to you, son. I love you more than anything and I only wanted you to have a normal life. I knew this would be hard for you and I couldn't do that to you. I just kept putting it off year after year until, after a while, I just couldn't bring myself to tell you. I didn't want to turn you against Tom and your dad. I just wanted everything to be normal and now I can't forgive myself for dropping this on you when I'm not there to answer your questions. You have every right to be mad at me for keeping this from you. I'm sorry. I don't expect you to forgive me and I just wish I could have done better for you while I had the chance.

I love you always, Mom.

"Noah?" Caroline almost whispers. "Are you okay?"

I can't do this. I can't sit here and talk to her about this like it's just something normal. I stand up and barely even notice when all the papers fall on the floor at my feet. I walk out of the office, get in my truck, and start driving.

I probably would have driven all the way back to Texas, but I wind up driving back to the ranch instead. I can't go into the house so I go down to the creek. The steers give me strange looks, but they don't stop me.

I squat down by the water and stare into the depths. This can't be right. Maybe she made a mistake and my dad really is my biological father. He has to be. I worshiped the ground my dad walked on. He was the man I always wanted to be.

I can't accept that my whole life was a lie, but maybe it wasn't. My dad raised me better than I could ever have hoped. He was always there and supported me as much as he supported Tom. My dad never let on even once that I wasn't his biological son.

I couldn't ask for better parents. My mom is right about that. She and my dad did everything anyone could ask to give me and Tom a perfect life. Maybe that's why she never told me. She didn't want to shatter the illusion. She wanted me to have as many good years as possible before I found out.

I stare into the water trying to wrap my head around all this when someone steps out of the trees. Caroline squats down next to me. She's wearing jeans, a t-shirt, and her sneakers. She looks so different, but in a way, she looks even more beautiful like this.

She squats down next to me and slips her hand under my arm. "How are you doing?"

I shrug and don't say anything. I can't look at her. This is not the way I wanted my day to go.

She rests her head on my shoulder and inches just a little bit closer to me so her body touches my side. "I brought your paperwork back. I put everything in your office."

I don't say anything. I should thank her. I should talk to her, but I can't. I don't even know who I am anymore.

What am I going to do when Tom finds out about this? What if he doesn't want to be in this business with me anymore because I'm not Sam Goldsmith's biological son? What if he and our cousins decide that I shouldn't inherit the family property because I have a different father? I dread finding out the answers to any of those questions.

Caroline snaps me out of my stupor by saying, "Would you like to go out with me next Saturday night?"

I spin around to stare at her. "I'd love to. Are we going back to the fair?"

"I thought we'd do something a little more traditional—like maybe go out to dinner."

"Okay." Now that I'm looking at her, I remember where I am and who it is that's hugging my arm. I dive in and kiss her. "Thanks. I'm sorry I walked out on you like that."

"You don't have to apologize. Anyone would be floored by that."

I look back into the water. "I just don't know what to do about any of this."

"You could start by notarizing all the paperwork your lawyer sent you. The letter is still under seal. You're the only person who knows the truth. You don't have to tell anyone until you're ready to—until all the title transfers go through. Legally, this shouldn't change anything."

I swallow hard. I've never been more grateful to anyone than I am to her for telling me this. She's right and it twists my heart that she can read me this easily.

"Thanks," I choke.

She hugs me tighter and kisses the side of my head. "This doesn't change anything, you know. The man you thought was your father

.....he loved you just as much. How much he loved you didn't change between yesterday and today."

I nod, but I can't speak. My throat hurts. I just want to make all of this go away. I want to wind back the clock to yesterday so I can go back to being Sam Goldsmith's real son.

She doesn't say anything for a long time until she kisses me again. "I know this is hard for you and I don't want to make it any harder, but there's something I have to tell you."

"Whatever it is, I don't want to know." I hear how harsh I'm being with her and I hate that, but I can't help it.

"You have to know. You need to know. I couldn't let you go without telling you. If I don't tell you now, you'll find out later when I'm not here and I need to be here with you when you find out. I can't let you find out alone."

"Fine," I growl. "What is it?"

She takes a deep breath. "After you left the office, I picked up all your papers and I was stacking them into a pile. I read your mother's letter, but there were other papers in there that you didn't see before you walked out. Sam Goldsmith's name is on your birth certificate. You're his son in every way that counts, so you have just as much legal claim to his property as your brother does."

"Good," I counter.

"There's more. Your mother included an old photograph of her and the man she met in San Diego. Your biological father is Ron Jamison, Hunter's father. That explains why you and Hunter look so much alike. You're brothers."

Chapter 8: Caroline

I take Noah's hand and pull him to his feet, but he still won't look at me. He keeps his eyes on the water bubbling over stones in the creek.

"Are you ready?"

He nods without saying anything. I can't let him stay in that terrible place alone.

I pivot in front of him so he has no choice but to look at me. "Let me help you. Let me be there for you."

His eyes meet mine at last, but they look unimaginably sad. "I am."

"Okay. Let's go."

I lead him up to his house and open the front door. It doesn't stink. In fact, the house looks practically new with all new beige carpets, matching curtains, and soft cream wallpaper. The house looks spectacular and a fresh pine-varnish smell comes from everywhere—that and the strong scent of roasting meat wafting from the kitchen.

I don't have time to congratulate Noah on what an outstanding job he did fixing up this place. I lead him to the back room that he's converted into his home office.

He collapses into his chair, buries his face in his hands, and groans when he sees his mother's letter on top of the stack of papers.

I hate to see him like this. He's usually so steady and easygoing. This is so hard for him. I rest my hand on his shoulder and turn over the sheets of paper. His birth certificate is in there and then we come to the picture of his mother Patricia with Ron Jamison outside the Port of San Diego. They look happy or at least cheerful.

Noah takes the picture out of my fingers and stares at it for a long time. I pull out my phone and scroll to one of the few pictures I still keep of Hunter. I hold it up for Noah to see and he takes my phone out of my hand.

He holds the two pictures side by side and stares at them. Ron doesn't resemble Hunter nowadays. Ron has aged and his wrinkles, grey hair, and hunched stature hide the resemblance.

It's much more noticeable in the picture. Ron looks like a younger version of Hunter....and Noah. It's so obvious now that I'm surprised I didn't think of it before. The three men look nearly identical except that Noah is bigger in the shoulders, taller, and slightly older than Hunter was in the picture.

All at once, he drops both the picture and my phone, pushes everything away from him, and collapses back in his chair. He turns his face away and his expression twists in a mixture of disgust and agony.

I have to do something to help him, but I don't know what to do. I squeeze his shoulder, and when that doesn't help, I run my fingers through his hair on the back of his head. I just want to be here for him in any way I can. I'd do anything to make this easier for him. I just don't know how.

He doesn't respond for a second and then he turns toward me. He still doesn't look at me when he wraps his arms around my waist and hugs his head into my stomach. I keep playing with his hair, rubbing his shoulders, and running my fingernails down his back. I don't know what else to do, and if holding me like this helps him, I can do that much.

He tightens his grip around me and turns his face into my stomach. He mouths across my midsection and crawls higher toward my breasts. I realize a second too late what he plans to do, and at that moment, both his big hands tighten on my ass.

The next instant, his mouth closes around my breast through my shirt. He bites, but not hard enough to hurt me. He uses just enough pressure to make me gasp in a sudden rush of hot passionate lust. How did this turn so quickly?

He sneaks his fingertips farther behind me, and in a split second, he's taking me there so fast that I can't stop my body from responding. His fingers slip between my legs from behind and he starts rubbing me through my jeans.

I grasp at his head trying to steady myself, but he's already nibbling my breasts through my shirt and pulling my legs apart even though I'm still standing up.

Without warning, he raises his head and kisses me. Before I know what hit me, we're kissing as never before. His tongue and lips light my blood on fire and my breath quickens with every delectable sweep of his tongue.

He rubs me so deep and hard that I feel myself getting wet from his attentions and I sway in his arms. He takes the hint and pulls me down on his lap in his chair. He guides my legs on either side of his lap and attacks me with both hands.

He pulls my hips tight against his rock-hard package and makes me moan. He kisses me so hard and so fast that he tips me over backward on his lap, and when I rock on his lap in spite of myself, he dives for my breasts.

I touch his cheeks and run my fingers through his hair rising on an unstoppable tide of desire. I want this. I want to do it with him and feel all the blissful pleasure from our date. I don't want to hold back anymore.

I haven't done it with anyone since Hunter died. This insatiable hunger won't be denied any longer.

He rears back, grabs my t-shirt, and pulls it over my head. Now only my bra separates him from my breasts and he goes to town. He pulls down one cup and his hot, crushing mouth sucks my nipple until I scream.

He flicks open my bra clasp and drops my bra on the floor. His shaft pulsates between my legs and makes me so fucking wild that I don't think I can stand waiting any longer. I ride down hard on it and he groans from the pressure.

I whine out of my mind when he sucks and plays with my breasts. I need to touch him. I need to feel all of him when he takes me. I tug up his shirt and he finally lets go long enough to rip it off over his head.

He lunges for me kissing me in insane fury. I can't keep up with him and every pinch of his fingers on my nipples makes me sob into his mouth.

He tears off panting hard, grabs me by the armpits, and lifts me onto his desk. In a split second, I'm sitting on the edge of his desk with my shirt off.

He starts unbuttoning my jeans and his eyes go hard and dangerous when he starts working my pants off. I can't look away from him when he drags them off, spreads my thighs, and buries his face in me.

He keeps groaning in satisfaction while he drives me to the stratosphere the way he did on our date. I can't stand this. I prop my arms back on his desk and convulse in rabid ecstasy when he stretches my legs apart so he can devour every torturous inch of me.

He fingers me until I explode in a screaming climax, but he isn't finished by a long way. His hard, determined eyes watch me from between my legs, and when he reduces me to a puddle of sobbing rapture, he leans back and starts unbuttoning his fly.

I need to do something more than just lie here and let him give me the greatest pleasure of my life. I need to give him something to show him how I feel about him. I need to let him know how much this means to me.

I try to sit up and wind up falling onto my knees in front of his chair. I bury my face in his fly and bite him through his jeans. He gasps the first time and then wilts with a tortured groan.

I love that sound and it gives me all the permission I need to pleasure him and take him to the stars. I nibble along his shaft through the thick canvas, and when I reach his fly, I breathe a deep breath of hot air into his shorts.

He pants and his throat catches when I nuzzle deeper into his pants. I take hold of his waistband and he sits up just enough for me to take his pants off.

I take him in my mouth and feel the blessed peaceful joy of giving him all the pleasure he just gave me. I love his fingertips digging into my shoulders and threading into my hair as I pick up speed. His muscles strain and his breathing becomes short and painful.

He sounds and smells and tastes different from Hunter. This is a completely different man with different desires and different pleasure spots. I can't suck him the same way I used to suck Hunter. I have to learn Noah from the beginning.

"Jesus, baby!" he rasps. "Oh, fuck, yes! What are you doing to me?"

I love hearing him talk like that. I love making him struggle to contain himself and his flesh pulsates in my mouth with every stroke.

All at once, he tightens his fist in my hair and pulls me off. He stares down into my eyes from above and a flood of excruciating desire seizes me.

He leans forward, hooks his hands under my armpits again, and lifts me back onto the desk. His eyes glint with brutal intensity when he pushes me back and pushes my knees apart.

He gets to his feet with his jeans down to his knees. His eyes leave me in no doubt about what he's going to do next. He bends over and plants his muscular arms on the desk on either side of me.

He starts kissing me slowly—so slowly that all my desire erupts even more than before. I need him so fucking bad. I need him right now, right here on his desk. I want him to think about doing it with me when he sits down here to work. I want him to get distracted thinking about me after I leave.

He leans so far forward that my shoulders almost come out of their sockets. I wrap my arms around his neck and slide the rest of the way to the edge of the desk. I want to get myself into the best position for him to take me to the limit.

I wrap my legs around his waist and pull him down. He flexes his hips to drive into me, but he doesn't actually do it. He strokes his length through my saturated tissues and teases me to screaming agony.

He never stops kissing me while his rigid manhood nudges me closer to the breaking point. I moan with every thrust, but no matter how much I twist my hips around, he still won't take me.

He reduces me to a sobbing wreck of anticipation before he straightens up, circles his arms behind my back, and lifts me off the desk. He sits back down in his chair with me still wrapped around him and pushes my hips back on his thighs just enough to work himself inside.

I collapse on top of him trembling all over as he slides home. He hugs me tight against his chest and now I can't stop the endless waves of pleasure and madness breaking over me.

My body takes over and I rock down hard on his shaft until it plunges all the way in. I hang onto him for dear life and try to scream, but his mouth muffles my cries. His hands close on my breasts before he crushes my ass in both hands.

He guides my movements into a fast, driving gallop for the finish line, but I'm already falling apart way too fast to stop. My head flops down on his shoulder and I can't stop screaming.

He grips the back of my neck and kisses the side of my face, my neck and shoulder, and down to my breasts. Everything he does spikes me into the heavens as I let madness take over. I can't stop it. This astronomical buried desire explodes out of control and I succumb completely into his hands.

I don't know what's happening to me when he closes both hands around my cheeks and picks up my head. I can't hold myself up and I surrender to this drunken ecstasy when he kisses me. I can't stop the crashing waves of climax tearing me apart as my body continues to throw me down on his spike.

He doesn't try to stop me. He arches his muscular body into me with every beat and his lips make me whimper with so much desire that I don't know what to do with myself.

I hear myself crying for him even though I already have him. I need something so much more, something more intense, something more delicious, something mind-blowingly fulfilling, but what's more mind-blowing than this?

He keeps contact with my cheek while we kiss as he wraps one arm behind my back. He slams me down impossibly hard, but every thrust only carries me higher on another wave of rapture. How is he doing this to me?

I notice the change in his noises first. He grunts once in what sounds like pain, scoots to the edge of his chair, and drives into me extra hard. He holds me there as a rippling pulse of tremors quakes through his whole body. I feel him throbbing inside me as he crumples in bliss.

He clamps his eyes shut tight and grimaces even as he keeps kissing me....and then he relaxes. He sinks back in his chair with me still strapped around his waist. He doesn't let me go and he pulls me down on top of him as we kiss.

Seeing him like this turns me on even more than I already was. I don't want this to end. I just want to keep doing this forever. I drape my body over his chiseled chest. I feel incredible right now, thanks to him.

I rock on him for as long as it lasts, but after a minute, our bodies wind down and start to relax.

He sighs and gives one last spasm before he opens his eyes. Those black gems glow with so much vitality and depth. I can't stop looking into them.

His hands glide up and down my body. He massages me and rubs everything and caresses every part of me just as attentively as he did before. He doesn't leave anything out. His attention makes me feel beautiful and attractive and desirable.....which is not something I'm used to.

He runs his fingertips down my cheek and combs strands of my hair behind my ears before he strokes my neck up my spine to my head. His eyes drill into my being searching for.....what is he looking for?

All at once, he bursts out laughing and his face lights up with boyish glee. "What?" I ask. "What's so funny?"

He won't stop snickering. "Let's not count this toward the hourly rate you're going to charge me for checking those papers."

I pretend to slap his shoulder. "Shut up! Don't be rude."

"I wasn't trying to be rude. I don't know why I'm laughing. It just came out."

I sit up, but I'm still straddling his waist in his office chair. I don't want to move even though we aren't doing anything anymore.

He doesn't try to make me get off. He beams at me from below and his warm, comforting hands keep exploring me with the same admiring strokes.

I sit up straight in front of him where he can see me, but he doesn't look any less pleased by what he sees. He keeps looking down at my breasts, my waist, my arms, my legs—he bestows the same glorious smile on every part of me.

"I should maybe get back to town," I tell him. "I have to pick up Dylan soon."

"Just don't tell your boss what you were doing out here." He starts laughing again. I try not to join in and end up laughing along with him.

"Are you gonna be okay?" I ask him.

"I'm fine now, thanks to you. Thank you for sticking around. This is the best medicine I could ask for." He chuckles and his hands close on my breasts.

He squeezes and I flinch as another surge of pleasure rushes through me. I groan and my eyes roll back in my head.

He pulls me down into his kiss and he keeps fondling me until I buzz with desire, but neither of us rises back to where we were before. We just rock in the slow, mellow rhythm of aching for each other.

He plays with my nipples until I whimper and whine. He rubs my back and neck, grips my hair, and shows every part of me the same blissful appreciation.

I open my eyes to find him looking down at me while we kiss. "Is there anything else you need me to do about this?" I ask.

"You've done enough. You've done more than I ever asked you to."

He stands up from his chair with me still latched onto him. He straightens up and holds me there attached to his chest while we kiss, but he can't touch me like this.

After a minute, gravity overcomes both our efforts to hold on. My legs fall down to the ground, I slide off him, and neither of us does anything to stop it.

We kiss for another eternity gazing into each other's eyes until, inevitably, we break apart. "Thanks for stopping by," he tells me and explodes in laughter.

I smirk and turn away to pick up my jeans. "Don't get used to it."

"No?" He bursts out laughing again. "You'd be welcome anytime you want to come over."

"Thanks, but if I did that, there would be no point in us going out on Saturday night."

"Of course there would be a point to it. We would still go out."

I make a face. "Who are you kidding? I would come over and we wouldn't leave the house until morning."

"Of course we would. I still want to go out with you."

I look up. "You do?"

"More than ever. I'd much rather go out with you than fool around with you here. I mean, I'd love to fool around with you here, but going out would be even better."

I feel my cheeks flushing and I try to hide it by putting on my pants. I don't want to think about what he means. Why would he want that unless he wants this to develop into more?

I pull on my jeans and he does the same thing while I put on my bra. "I was thinking...."

"Be careful," he teases.

"Stop it. I was thinking I could invite the Jamisons over to my place. You could come over and we could break the news.... if you want to."

"I appreciate you suggesting it because I wasn't sure if I should. It would be kind of nice to get to know.....my father."

"I'm sure he would love to get to know you. He was devastated when Hunter died."

"I'm not Hunter," he growls.

"I know and I'm sure he knows it, too. It's just that....you're his son, just like Hunter was. He lost his son. Now he's about to find out that he has another one.... if you want to. I understand if you don't. I won't tell them if you don't want me to."

"No, I'd like to. Thank you."

"Of course." I rise on my tiptoes and kiss him on the cheek. "I gotta go. Why don't you come into the office tomorrow and we'll finish notarizing the rest of your title transfers?"

Chapter 9: Noah

I fidget on the sidewalk trying to get my clothes to feel comfortable again. Maybe I should have worn a tie for this meeting, but that would probably make me even more nervous.

There's a strange car parked outside Caroline's house. It must belong to the Jamisons, which means they're already here. They're inside shooting the breeze with Caroline and playing around with Dylan. They have no idea what's about to happen to them.

I almost hate to do to them what my mom did to me, but they have to find out sooner or later. I need to get to know this Ron Jamison that is my biological father. There's no better way to do that than to tell him face to face and at least Caroline will be there. She's their other son's former wife. She'll be able to smooth over the hysteria that is bound to ensue.

I jump a foot in the air when my phone pings, but it's just an email notification. It isn't as important as what I'm about to do, but it snaps me out of my trance and I head up to the front porch.

I ring the doorbell and Caroline answers. She lets me in and shuts the door behind me.

I hear Dylan laughing and the two would-be grandparents talking to him in the background. I was right about them interacting with him. They treat him like a grandson even though he's a donor baby.

She leads me into the living room and Claire Jamison goes as white as a sheet when she sees me. I try to smile down at her. "Good morning, Mrs. Jamison."

She gulps. "Good morning."

"Take a seat, Noah," Caroline tells me. "Can I get you something to drink?"

"No, thanks. I'm good."

The two old people eye me across the coffee table where they're helping Dylan build something out of Legos. He doesn't notice anything strange except that he doesn't know who I am.

Caroline pulls up a chair next to me and inhales a deep breath. "Ron—Claire—some of Noah's family documents have just come to light and it turns out that his mother Patricia lived in San Diego before she married Noah's dad."

Ron's head whips around so fast he almost gives himself whiplash. His expression goes blank and he stares at me in horror.

"Noah's mother was Patricia Ainsley. You knew her, didn't you, Ron? She died last year and she left Noah a letter stating that she got pregnant the night you spent in San Diego. She never told anyone and her husband Sam raised Noah as his own. No one knew until just a few days ago."

Ron's eyes lock onto me with so much power that I can't look away. The room goes deadly quiet except for Dylan still messing with his Legos.

"Noah has documentation that his mother left him in her will." Caroline bumps my elbow, and when I jolt out of my trance, she waves at the folder in my hand. "Show them."

I scramble to open the folder and hand the letter and the picture across the table. Ron takes them and sits there staring at the picture for a long time. I feel myself shaking waiting for lightning to strike. Is he going to laugh me out of the room? Is he going to deny meeting my mom in San Diego all those years ago?

He finally raises his eyes to meet mine and I see them swimming with tears. "My son!" he croaks. "My son!"

"HOW COULD YOU DO THIS TO ME?!" his wife shrieks and leaps out of her seat. She rounds on her husband screeching to wake the dead—literally. "You bastard! You traitor! You disloyal, lying, traitorous asshole!"

He starts to get out of his seat and drops both the letter and the picture on the coffee table. "Honey—sweetheart—darling—!"

"Don't you dare come near me!" she roars. "You lying, traitorous bastard! How could you do this to me? How could you not tell me? I trusted you!"

She whirls away and gets halfway across the living room before Ron lunges for her, grabs her elbow, and pulls her to a stop. "I'm sorry, sweetheart! I didn't know! She never told me. It was one night years before I ever met you. I never would have kept this from you if I knew the truth. Just...." His eyes swivel back toward me and the same look of deep, aching need grabs me again.

"You called him your son!" she bellows. "How could you do that to Hunter? How could you betray our whole family....with *him*?!" She aims a threatening finger at me and then spins away on her heel.

She charges out of the house and the front door slams behind her. Ron watches her with trembling lips and then he turns back to me.

He extends one hand to me and opens his mouth to say something before he changes his mind. His whole countenance slumps in defeat and despair and he lets his arm fall. "I better go after her."

Caroline goes over to him and squeezes his arm. "You couldn't have known. You didn't do anything wrong."

"I should have known," he murmurs. "I should have…. done something. I better go." He shoots me one last heart-wrenching glance and walks out of the house.

This turned out to be almost as big a disaster as I expected. I just wish Ron could have stuck around a little longer so I could talk to him, but I guess that's never going to happen now.

Dylan scrutinizes me a little too closely when I pick up my mom's letter and picture. I put them back in my folder. "I better go. Thanks for trying."

Caroline grabs my arm next. "You don't have to go. Don't go home if you're too upset about this. Why don't you stay for dinner?"

"What's for dinner, Mommy?" Dylan interrupts.

"You know what's for dinner, darling," she tells him. "We always have enchiladas on Saturday night."

"Enchiladas, huh?" I reply. "I'm from Texas, you know. I can be very particular when it comes to my Mexican food."

She blushes and grins at me. "I think I can meet even your exacting standards."

"All right. You convinced me. Now I have to taste these world-famous enchiladas for myself."

Dylan looks up at me. "Who are you?"

He asks so innocently and with such obvious, childish curiosity that I find myself smiling at him. "I just moved into town."

"Oh." He goes back to working on his Legos, all his curiosity satisfied with that one simple explanation.

Caroline touches my arm. "Why don't you sit down and make yourself at home? I'll bring you something to drink."

"Thanks."

She beams at me with a huge, warm smile, goes to the kitchen, and I sit down on the couch. I bend over the table and start fitting the Legos together. "What are you making?"

"This is a dinosaur." Dylan holds up a rectangle of several small Legos put together into one block.

I nod trying to decide what to say. "What kind is it? I like T-rex best. Which dinosaur is your favorite?"

"T-rex," he replies.

I smile in approval. "Good choice. Maybe we could make a Pteranodon, too."

He frowns at me trying to figure out what I'm talking about. He doesn't know what a Pteranodon is—not that it matters. I'm talking to a two-year-old.

I fit some random Legos together not trying to make anything in particular and Dylan does the same thing. We don't need to talk now that we're united in our mutual interest in Legos.

Caroline comes back and places a glass of iced tea on a coaster at my elbow. It has a slice of lemon and a sprig of mint in it. I frown at the glass while she starts setting the dining room table. How did she know how I like my iced tea? I can't remember ever mentioning it to her.

She finishes setting the table and a mouth-watering smell of chili, spices, and toasted cheese makes me look up when she brings the tray of enchiladas from the kitchen. She catches me looking and grins when she puts it in the middle of the table.

She comes over to the table and picks up Dylan. He kicks up a fuss and tries to contort out of her arms to get back to his Legos, but he changes his tune when she puts him in his highchair and starts buckling a bib around his neck.

I carry my tea over to the table and she waves at the seat opposite hers and Dylan's. "Sit over there where you'll be out of the firing line of flying beans and shrapnel. You're about to go behind enemy lines into dangerous kid territory."

I laugh. "I'm used to it. My brother Tom has three kids. Going over to their house for Sunday dinner was like the D-Day invasion at Normandy."

She laughs along with me. "Do you have any other siblings?"

"No, it's just the two of us."

I sit down where she told me and put my tea next to my plate. She takes my plate and serves me a big steaming sloppy pile of enchiladas that smell like nothing I've ever smelled in my life.

She adds rice, beans, and salad to my plate, hands it back to me, and cuts up some enchiladas into Dylan's much smaller bowl.

He starts scooping the food into his mouth and I start eating while she serves herself. "Do you usually eat like this when it's just the two of you?" I ask.

"No way! This was for Ron and Claire....and there's another tray of enchiladas in the kitchen. You can take it home with you if you want."

"Really?" I take a bite of the food. "You're hired."

She laughs. "Most single guys don't eat very well."

"You're right. It isn't easy to get motivated to cook when it's just me alone in that house."

"So....do you have any prospects for your future wife?"

My head snaps up, but I relax when I see her grinning at me. "I might have a few applicants for the position."

"A few!" She giggles. "Wow, what a player!"

I join in the joke and eat some more. These enchiladas are mind-blowingly incredible. I am definitely going to have to bump her up to the top of the list of potentials if she can cook like this. Granted, she's the only woman on the list at the moment, but this is just another point in her favor.

She keeps getting distracted by Dylan's eating habits which aren't nearly as bad as my nieces' and nephews'. He's actually quite well house-broken and he keeps casting curious glances at me across the table.

"How did you learn to cook like this?" I ask.

She smiles at me and then bends over her plate blushing like anything. "You never asked me where I came from. I grew up in San Antonio. We ate like this all the time when I was growing up."

"That explains how you knew about the tea," I remark.

"Something like that."

"Thank you for inviting me." I look around the table at this little family. It might be small, but it's pretty nice. "It's great to have a home-cooked meal in a real home. I didn't think moving away from my family would be this hard."

"You're only saying that because of all this other stuff that happened," she replies. "Anyway, I'm glad we could help you out. You should come over more often if your house is feeling too lonely."

I don't answer, but I can't help checking out everything about her house while I eat. It's really comfortable and I enjoy her company.

Just when I start to think I might have found a little slice of heaven on Earth, Dylan starts to fuss. He bangs his spoon on the table, and when Caroline tries to intervene, he throws his spoon across the room.

He narrowly misses my head and it hits the wall behind me. Caroline pounces on him and takes his bowl away from him. "If you aren't eating, it's time to leave the table."

He goes ballistic and tries to snatch the bowl back from her. He manages to grab the rim and comes perilously close to yanking it out of her hand before she overpowers him and moves it out of his reach.

"All right, pal. You're all done." She stands up and starts moving him away from the table and taking him out of his chair. "It sounds like it's time for bed."

"I want my dinner!" he roars. "I want my dinner!"

She gets him halfway across the room and stops with him writhing in her arms. "Will you sit quietly and eat nicely? If you don't, I'm taking you away."

"I want my dinner!" he yells. "I want my dinner!"

She pulls the highchair back to the table, but the instant she brings the bowl near him, he makes a dive and tries to grab the food with his bare hand.

She rips him away so fast he doesn't know what hit him. He tries one last desperate lunge for the bowl, but she knuckles down with merciless determination, rolls her eyes at me, and hauls the offender out of the room.

He shrieks all the way and I have to chuckle when I hear her balling him out in the other room. "You know you aren't allowed to eat like that at the dinner table, Dylan. You sit nicely in your chair and eat your food or you leave the table. That's the rule. Now come on. It's time to put on your pajamas."

I have all the time I want to finish my enchiladas and there is no way in Hell I'm leaving without that second tray. These are fantastic.

I listen to their interaction as she gets him ready for bed and then sings to him before she puts him to bed. She's a much better mother than even I suspected. She's tough, consistent, and kind. She never loses her temper with her son.

I'm impressed and she's definitely earning my respect as I get to know her better. She's been doing this alone for two years. That's a tall order and she does it so well.

She comes back almost half an hour later and sinks down into her chair across from me. "Sorry about that."

"Nothing to be sorry about. Eat your dinner."

She sighs and takes a bite. "Thanks. Do you need anything?"

"I'm fine. Is it usually like this?"

"All the time."

I chuckle. "He'll grow up.... someday. I don't think he'll eat like this when he's twenty-five."

She laughs. "I hope not. I'm sorry things didn't work out too well with the Jamisons."

"Either way, I had to tell them....or for you to tell them. Ron had to know and maybe it isn't finished working itself out. Maybe it will work itself out better in the future."

"We can hope so. Claire was pretty upset."

"I can't blame her and I didn't expect either of them to handle it very well. At least she didn't call *me* a liar and a traitor and a bastard."

"She couldn't, could she? You didn't do any of this."

"Thank you for handling this for me," I tell her. "I don't think I would have had the nerve to actually say the words out loud. I'm grateful that you did it for me."

She shrugs. "Sure. Whatever you need."

I wipe the enchilada sauce off my mouth. "I should probably get out of here. I didn't mean to move in."

She bursts into a huge grin, and before I can move, she slides her hand across the table to mine. "Do you want to spend the night?"

"You mean....?" I glance down the hall toward Dylan's room. It's all quiet.

"I understand if you don't want to."

"Of course I want to," I reply. "Are you sure?"

"Absolutely. Did you think I wasn't?"

I don't know what to say and she doesn't give me a chance. She stands up and starts clearing the table. She takes her plate and Dylan's to the kitchen followed by the half-eaten tray of enchiladas and all the leftovers.

She comes around to my side of the table to take my plate and a charge of adrenaline goes through me when she comes near me. I get a flashback of her riding my lap in my office at home.

I would love to pull her down on my lap right now and take her right here at the dining room table. I would love to strip her naked and take her right out in the middle of her house where anyone would be able to see her if anyone was here.

She didn't ask that, though. She asked me to spend the night and that gives me so many other wild ideas.

I stand up and pull her in to kiss her. Her lips soften instantly and she falls into my arms so effortlessly that my insides squirm. I can't wait to get my hands on her.

Her eyes glisten when I finally lean back to gaze into her eyes. Her countenance glows with so much suppressed heat. She's so passionate and accessible. I love making her look up at me like that—like she knows exactly what I'm thinking and she wants it as much as I do.

I step away from the table and she gets busy clearing the rest of the table. I wander around the living room looking at everything while she puts everything in the kitchen.

Pictures of her and Dylan cover a shelf along one wall. They look happy and they obviously love each other. She's so responsible and straightforward. She handles her own business without a hint of complaint. She just takes the horse by the reins and steers her life where she wants it to go.

I imagine what it would be like if we were living together—either here or somewhere else. She would be clearing the table like this, and when she finished, we would go to our bedroom and spend the night together.

Time blurs and I imagine that we're already doing that. I'm her husband and she's my wife. That's our son asleep in the other room and this is our home.

She comes back and starts scooping the Legos into a tote that she keeps in the corner, but I stop her and pull her back into my arms.

She collapses into my kiss and her body shivers with tension when I stroke her sides and start playing with her breasts. She wraps her arms around my neck and presses her body into me.

She doesn't pull away when she feels how hard I am. She sinks down on her heels, takes my hand, leads me down the hall to her bedroom, and shuts the door behind her.

Chapter 10: Caroline

I jolt wide awake when the alarm goes off on my phone. I have to flounder out of a sound sleep to reach my phone and Noah's burly arm around my ribs doesn't make it easier.

He doesn't move, and when I turn off the alarm and collapse on the bed, he pulls me close and nuzzles into me from behind. He burrows his face deeper into my hair and hugs me against him.

His breathing lengthens right away. He's falling back to sleep, but I don't have that option. I touch his wrist where it crosses my stomach. "I have to get up."

He grunts something under his breath and instantly starts breathing deeply again. I wait, but he doesn't move.

"You might work for yourself, but I don't," I tell him. "I have to get up."

He doesn't respond at all this time. Is he even awake enough to realize what I'm saying?

I have to get up, take a shower and get dressed, and be out of this room before Dylan wakes up. I have to be ready to make his breakfast, get him dressed, and be ready to walk out the door to take him to daycare. All of that takes time.

Noah's heavy, chiseled arm holds me down on the bed. I don't want to get up. I want to stay in bed with him all day, but some of us have jobs.

I twist over under his arm and he groans when I snuggle up to him facing him this time. His lips don't move and he doesn't open his eyes when I kiss him. This can't continue so I fall back on the one thing I know for certain will get a response from him.

I shove him onto his back and climb on top of him. I rub my breasts against his broad chest and glide my crotch over him under the covers. I grind on him until I feel him starting to get hard. Then I start kissing him again.

He moans when I nudge him to full hardness and then slide down on top of him. I stay stretched out on him while I swim in this sea of pleasure synchronizing our bodies into one.

He grabs my ass and crams me down on him. He's definitely awake now. I push myself up on my arms while my body still holds him in that rhythm. "I have to go to work now."

"Do you have to?" He cracks one eye open. "Stay here."

"Dylan will wake up in half an hour. Stay in here, and when I take him to daycare, you can leave."

He sighs again when I corkscrew my hips on him. "What will you do if I stay here and wait for you to get home from work?"

I laugh. "You have a business to run, remember?"

"Don't remind me," he growls.

I slide off him and stay there on my hands and knees while we kiss. He starts playing with my breasts again. I can't let him tempt me to get back into bed, so I get up and head for the shower. "I'll leave the enchiladas on the counter for you."

I take a shower, and when I get out to get dressed, Noah is lying propped up in bed messing with his phone. "Come here, baby," he tells me.

I sit on the edge of the bed and kiss him, but when he slides his hand up my legs under my skirt, Dylan calls from down the hall, "Mommy!"

I tear myself away and hear Noah chuckling behind me as I go to get my son up for the day. I go through the rest of my routine, and right before I take Dylan out to the car, I return to the bedroom to kiss Noah goodbye.

"I loved having you here last night," I whisper.

"I loved being here. Does that mean we can do it again?"

"I'd love to. Text me, okay?"

I hurry away and I don't even worry about leaving a naked guy in my bedroom. I almost wish he will be here waiting for me when I get home tonight.

I drop Dylan off at daycare and I make it quick so I don't have to answer any awkward questions from Willow. Don't ask me how I'm going to break the news to her or anyone else about me and Noah....or anything else.

I get to the office in time and sit down at my desk to find a new appointment on my calendar for Noah to come in and notarize all his title transfer documentation. That meeting can't possibly go any worse than the last one.

I turn to a few more leads from Tim and inquiries from potential buyers who want to view properties around town. I get through most of the morning when my phone rings. *Unknown Caller.*

I answer it. "Caroline Hirsch speaking."

"Good morning, Ms. Hirsch," a woman's voice replies. "This is Lieutenant Maggie Keller. I'm with the Department of Defense dealing with survivor benefits for active servicepeople killed while members of the Armed Forces."

"Hi," I reply. "What is this about? I already receive Hunter's benefits."

"Yes, Ma'am," she replies. "It appears that there is a separate Survivor Benefits Program account in your name that we weren't aware of until recently—which is why I'm contacting you."

"What other account?" I ask. "I went through all this with the Navy after Hunter's death. All the accounts paid out at the time."

"Yes, Ma'am, all the accounts that were known were paid out at the time. This account was not known. We only just discovered it. Anyway, it pays out the usual fifty-five percent of the deceased serviceperson's retirement pay, which amounts to approximately thirty thousand dollars per year adjusted for inflation for the duration of the beneficiary's life."

The amount staggers my mind, but the way she says this makes me prick up my ears. "What do you mean—for the duration of the beneficiary's life? Who would be the beneficiary if not me?"

"It appears that your son Dylan is the named beneficiary since he would be your late husband's next of kin...."

"Hold it right there," I interrupt. "Dylan is not Hunter's next of kin. Dylan is not Hunter's son. I conceived using donor sperm three years after Hunter's death. Dylan shouldn't be mentioned on any of Hunter's records."

"Really? Hmmm." She hesitates. "That's strange. We must have an error in our records."

"It sounds like it."

"Anyway," she chirps, "we would need to see documentation of that. Otherwise, the benefit will be paid out to Dylan regardless since that is what is on our records."

"Documentation—of what?" I don't want to know.

"Documentation of Dylan's parentage. We would need to see DNA results or any other records you can provide on your date of conception...."

"He's only two years old!" I fire back. "Please tell me you have his date of birth on record. How do you think I conceived three years after Hunter's death? It's biologically impossible that Hunter could be Dylan's father."

"We would still need to see documentation submitted to our office, Ma'am. I apologize for the inconvenience. Otherwise, we'll just go ahead with the benefit payments to your usual receiving bank account...."

I get off the phone as quickly as possible and grind my teeth. The US Military isn't the most efficient organization in the world, but this really reaches new heights of ridiculous.

What in the holy hell are they doing paying out survivor benefits to a child who was born three years after the serviceperson's death? It makes no sense at all. I can't imagine what documentation I could provide that would offer more conclusive proof than Dylan's date of birth.

I'll just have to contact the sperm bank and get their records of my purchase, though I don't know what good that will do. I don't even know if the sperm bank keeps DNA records on their donors, and if they do, and if they give me a DNA profile on my donor, I would have to get a DNA test on Dylan.

I go home on my lunch break. Noah is gone and there's a note on the counter in place of the tray of enchiladas I left out for him. *Thanks. XX.*

I smile at it and then go to my desk in the corner of the living room. I start going through my files and pull out everything I still have from when I purchased the donor sperm. It seems so long ago. I can hardly remember what my life looked like without Dylan in it.

The donor profile doesn't include any identifying information. It uses a number in place of the donor's name. The description doesn't give much information, either. It says he has brown hair, brown eyes, and that he's a college student studying engineering. That's why I chose him. I thought another engineer would be as close as I was going to get to Hunter.

The profile lists his hobbies as hiking, wrestling, and bowling. He could be anyone. He's completely anonymous, which I guess is kind of the point, isn't it?

I kept the receipt from my purchase, but time has eroded the ink and the receipt is unreadable. I can barely make out the date, so I call the sperm bank.

A dreary, bored, depressed female voice answers the phone. "Banner Falls Sperm Bank, you're speaking with Bethany. How can I help you today?"

"Hi, Bethany," I reply. "I purchased some sperm from you about two and a half years ago and I was wondering if I could get another copy of my receipt and any other documentation related to my purchase."

"May I have your surname?" she drawls.

I give it and she starts reading my file. "Caroline?"

"Yes!" I practically yell.

She reads back my email address and agrees to send through all the receipts and information on my purchase—not that I hold out much hope that it will make a difference. I might just have to grit my teeth and accept another thirty thousand dollars in government benefits every year if I can't find a way to prove that Dylan was born after Hunter's death.

I head back to the office, and when I park my car in the parking lot, I get an email notification. I read the PDF from the sperm bank on the way into the office and I can hardly believe I'm dealing with the same organization.

The sperm bank has completely changed their whole profile system and I stop dead in my tracks when I see the donor's picture staring back at me. The donor's name stands out across the top of the profile. It's Noah Goldsmith.

Chapter 11: Noah

My stomach flips when I look out of my office window and see Caroline's car pull into my driveway. That was quick. She just can't keep away from me. I knew my personality was irresistible, but this woman is electric.

I go out on the porch to greet her and my blood runs cold when I see her get out of the car. She slams the door extra hard and stands next to the vehicle scowling at me with exactly the same expression she used that first morning when I met her right here in front of this house.

She holds a folder of papers in one hand, and after she glares at me for a minute, she turns aside and presses her hand to her forehead in exactly the same way. What's the matter with her? Something must have happened since she left me in her bedroom just a few hours ago.

I walk out to meet her. She wears the same clothes she had on when she left for work this morning. She must have come straight from the office.

I straighten up in front of her. "You okay? Do you want to come inside?"

She doesn't blink. She keeps scowling at me like she didn't even hear me. "I need to talk to you. It's serious."

"Okay. Do you want to talk here or do you want to come inside?"

She looks away and compresses her lips. "I don't care."

"Come inside."

I lead her up the steps to the front door, but I don't take her hand. I don't want to know whatever it is that turned her against me. It was nice while it lasted.

I hesitate when I get inside. I don't want to take her to my office, so I settle for the kitchen. That should be relatively neutral ground. We've never done it there.

She scrutinizes the kitchen while I go over to the fridge. "I don't have any iced tea," I tell her. "Do you want some iced coffee instead?"

She slaps down the folder on the counter in front of me. "Take a look at this."

I don't like the way she's acting at all. This whole situation feels like a trap. I flip back the cover of the folder....and the bomb goes off in my face—the face staring back up at me from my file from the sperm bank.

It's all there—my time studying engineering in college—my interests—even my name and address.

"The sperm bank changed its protocol after I bought the sperm that I used to conceive," she tells me in a raspy voice. "When I bought the sperm, there was nothing there but a number and a few words about your hair and eye color. They changed last year so that donors and purchasers could know each other. It's some new initiative to allow children conceived by egg and sperm donation to contact their donors. I swear I didn't know. You have to believe me. I didn't know it was you. I never would have...."

Her voice gets progressively more strained as she talks faster and faster. She finally chokes off at the end and covers her mouth.

I can't stop staring at the file. Is this really happening? Is she saying what I think she's saying?

She sniffs. "Please say something," she moans. "I'm so sorry for doing this to you. I had no idea. Please believe me. I never knew about any of this until....I had to...."

I stagger away feeling.....I feel like I'm going to fall over. I stumble over to the sink, prop my arms on the counter, and wobble on my watery knees for a second. "Are you saying.....?" I straighten up and wind up looking across the property to the creek in the distance. "Are you saying.....that Dylan....is mine?"

"I'm so sorry, Noah!" Now I can hear that she's crying. She keeps apologizing to me as though this is a bad thing. "I didn't know! I'm so sorry!"

"Are you saying.....?" I can't say the words.

That little boy—the Legos—the T-rex—the enchiladas—is this really happening?

He's mine. He's my.....I don't want to let myself think that word. My world teeters on its axis and it doesn't come back to standing up straight again. It never will.

My son. I have a son. That little boy is mine. I'm his father.

I've been trying to find a woman to marry so I could have my own kids. I've been trying to start a family, and all this time, that little boy was growing up and throwing tantrums and making T-rexes out of Legos and going to daycare without me.

Caroline closes the folder, picks it up, and runs her hand across her face. "I'll leave you alone. I'm really sorry about this. I'll just...."

I cross the kitchen in half a second, and before I even think about it, she's in my arms. She bursts into tears against my shirt, but I don't care. I have her. That's enough.

I hold her while she cries, and when she finishes, I run cold water on a washcloth and hand it to her.

"I'm so sorry!" she groans.

"Stop it," I tell her. "Of course you didn't know."

She gulps and her features spasm. "What are we gonna do about this?"

"What do you want to do about it?"

She shrugs. "I don't know what there is to do about it."

"Well, you got pregnant because you planned to raise him alone. If you want to keep raising him alone, that's your decision."

She gapes at me with her mouth open. "Are you insane? Do you really think I'd keep him from you?"

"He's a donor baby. How much I have to do with him is entirely up to you."

"But...you want to know him, don't you? Of course you do. You want kids. You wouldn't be satisfied to stay in the background. You would want to know him and for him to know you. You would want as much to do with him as you could get."

"Of course I would, but that's your decision. It isn't like you could just drop me on him out of the clear blue sky."

"Will you stop it?!" she practically shrieks. "He's two years old! What better time is there for him to get to know you? If you're going to be in his life, now is the perfect time to introduce you. You could be in his life from now on and he would never know any difference. He probably wouldn't even remember meeting you for the first time. You would just always be there. You would be his....his dad."

She bursts into tears again and I fold her in my arms. Those words make me want to cry, too. I'm a father. My son. I can't believe I'm even thinking that.

Seeing her fall apart somehow makes me so much stronger, though. I don't need to break down because she's doing it for both of us. I can be strong for both of us.

I let her go when I hear her slowing down. I sit down on a stool by the counter, run her washcloth under the tap, and hand it to her. She presses it to her eyes and sniffs.

"So...." she begins again. "How do you want to do this?"

"How do *you* want to do this?"

She nods and throws back her head. "How about you come over for dinner again? You can get to know him and you two can....spend some time together."

"Okay. Thank you."

She looks up at me with her brimming eyes. "I'm......" Her face wrenches in agony. "I'm glad it's you."

She completely falls apart again and I don't get off my stool when I pull her into my arms. I draw her sideways onto my lap and hold her while she sobs.

She finally straightens up and reaches for her washcloth again. Her eyes are puffy and bloodshot now, but she looks immaculately beautiful now that I know she's crying for me. She's crying because the last wall is falling down between us.

I pet her cheeks and comb her hair out of her eyes and rub her back while she pulls herself together. She scowls without even trying to look happy. She looks like this is the most devastating catastrophe ever.

Seeing her like this makes me.....happy. I don't know why. I have a son....and I have her. She doesn't stop me from comforting her about this.

She said she's glad it's me and we're already together. I don't have to wonder about that anymore. I spent last night in her bed with my arms around her. We're together....and we have a son together.

I don't know how all of this is going to work, but it doesn't really matter. It's good no matter what happens. If she decides to continue to raise Dylan alone—if I keep living here and seeing Dylan on the weekends—what difference does it make?

I'll still be in his life. He'll grow up knowing who I am exactly the way she said. She said it. She insists on it. She wants me in his life, which is a dream come true for me. Whatever else happens doesn't mean a damn thing.

She glances over at me with her blazing red eyes. "Sorry."

"You don't have to apologize to me. I'm glad you told me."

"I mean I'm sorry for falling apart on you like this. I'm not sorry that you're the donor. I'm just.... I don't know how to deal with this. I don't know what my life is going to look like if you....."

"I understand," I tell her when she doesn't finish. "You have every right to fall apart. This isn't what you signed up for. It isn't what I signed up for, either, but it's still a good thing. I'm happy about it."

"You are?"

"Of course. This is a dream come true for me."

"About us......."

I don't want her to finish. I don't want to hear whatever it was she was going to say after that. I dive in and kiss her, and once I start, I just can't stop.

I pick her up planning to take her to my bedroom, but I only make it as far as the hall before I stop and put her down. I have to have her right here and now. I push her up against the wall and she meets me just as intensely.

She kisses me fast and deep and hot, but that only sets me off. I crush her against the wall pulling up her legs on either side of my hips. I need her so fucking bad I can't stand it.

I arch into her to take her right here, but a second later, her unbelievable energy takes over. She drops her legs and turns her back to me. I can't stand that and I drive into her so fucking hard I don't even know what I'm doing anymore.

I can't stop mouthing her neck, her cheek, her shoulder—every part of her that I can reach while our bodies explode in a hurricane tempest that just won't stop.

Chapter 12: Caroline

My pulse quickens when I hear the knock at the door. This is a whole different level of nerves and excitement. Dylan doesn't even notice when I leave the room and go to answer the door.

Noah looks just as nervous as I feel and he keeps rubbing his hands together and down his legs. I slip out onto the porch, put my arms around him, and kiss him, but he breaks off almost immediately. "I don't know if I can do this."

"Sure, you can," I tell him. "You were made for this."

"Maybe not. Maybe I'm not cut out to be a father."

"Of course you are. You wouldn't want to be a father this much as you do if you weren't cut out for it."

"What if I fuck up?" He glances behind me even though the door is shut. "What if I make his life worse than it would be without me in it?"

I laugh, but I'm just as anxious as he is. "You will fuck up. That's Rule #1 of being a parent. You'll fuck up and you'll fuck up big time. You can't be a perfect parent no matter how much you might like to be."

"Maybe I shouldn't, then."

"Yes, you should. Come on. You don't have to give him any meaningful pearls of wisdom. He doesn't even know you. Just sit there and let him see you. That's all you're doing. Just be there."

"Are you sure?" He shuffles his feet some more. "It can't be that simple."

I have to kiss him. He's so sweet and he cares so much. He just wants to do the right thing and that's what makes him the perfect father. "Come on. Just come inside and we'll take it from there."

I take his hand and lead him back to the living room. "Dylan, Noah's here to have dinner with us again."

Dylan looks up, sees Noah, and holds up a cube of Legos with two vertical pieces sticking out on both sides. "T-rex!"

Noah gives the very smallest of smiles. "Yeah. It is. It's so lifelike, too. You're a genius."

I push him toward the couch and he pivots around the coffee table to sit down in the same place as last time.

I back off to watch the fireworks. Noah starts playing with the Legos in between shooting sidelong glances at Dylan. Dylan doesn't even look at him until he makes another knobbled ball of Legos with two sticks poking out the bottom. "It's a dinosaur!"

"Which kind?" Noah asks. "It kind of looks like Triceratops, don't you think?"

Dylan screws up his forehead and frowns at. "What's that?"

"It was a big, ugly dinosaur with three horns sticking out of its head.....like this." Noah selects three long, thin Legos and clips them to the ball to form horns. It looks more like a Triceratops now except that it doesn't have any body or legs.

Dylan stares at it and then bursts into loud laughter. He jumps up and starts flying the Triceratops around the room. He makes zooming noises with his mouth and swoops it close to the other Legos before flying off somewhere else.

Noah laughs and says, "Triceratops didn't fly, buddy."

Dylan completely ignores him and Noah goes back to playing with his Legos. He starts building a tower, and after a minute, Dylan notices and comes back over. He discards his Triceratops and starts building something else.

I have to summon all my willpower to tear myself away. Watching them makes me so happy. I got pregnant knowing I would never be able to give Dylan a father. Now he has one. He doesn't even know the priceless treasure that just dropped into his lap.

I couldn't ask for a better man than Noah to be Dylan's father. I'm not even sure anymore if Hunter would be a better father. Noah takes being a father so seriously. It's everything he's ever wanted and he'll do anything to make it work.

I know it's true when he looks at Dylan. Noah's eyes well up with so much emotion. He can't believe his good fortune that he has a son. Gratitude overflows my heart when I think of the circumstances that brought me to this point.

I set the table with a glass of iced tea at Noah's place and I bring out the meatloaf, mashed potatoes, and steamed buttered green beans. I hate to interrupt Noah and Dylan when it comes time to call them to dinner.

They've formed two separate towers and Noah is talking Dylan through the delicate construction of a causeway connecting the two structures. "We need something to brace it up over here," he tells Dylan. "We should add some Legos underneath right here to act as support girders."

I burst out laughing. "Never play Legos with an engineer."

Noah looks up and breaks into a grin when he sees me watching him. "I can't help it. It's just the way my brain works."

"How did you become a rancher?" I pick up Dylan and put him in his highchair. "What made you quit?"

"My dad died. He had twelve different properties all running cattle and he had a staff of managers running the whole operation. My brother Tom was going to take over the business after my dad died while I stayed in my lonely office designing buildings and bridges."

"Did you really? Is that what you did?"

"I loved it. It was my dream job, but it became obvious pretty quick that Tom couldn't do everything by himself so I took a break from engineering to help him get on top of things. One thing led to another and I just kind of stayed on."

"Don't you want to go back?" I ask. "Don't you miss engineering?"

"I might still go back. We'll see what happens....or I might just live vicariously through Legos." He turns to look down at Dylan and notices the meatloaf. "What—no Mexican food? I'm disappointed."

"I'll make Mexican food on the side whenever you come over, but certain people need to eat the same thing on the same nights of the week. Their tiny brains can't handle the unpredictability of too much variety."

"I understand." Noah sits down opposite us and watches me put on Dylan's bib. "You don't have to make anything different for me. I was just fooling around. Don't read too much into it."

I serve him and then I serve Dylan and myself. Dylan stares back and forth between Noah and me taking in our conversation and he doesn't make a scene when he starts eating. He just stuffs the food into his mouth while he keeps looking back and forth between me and Noah.

He's behaving so well that I take a chance and turn to Noah while we both eat. "Have you thought any more about telling your family about....you know what?"

"I haven't decided. I've been thinking more and more that I might just follow my mom's example and never say anything. I mean, I understand why she eventually had to tell me, but what would it actually do for Tom and his family to find out? It would accomplish absolutely nothing except to maybe tear our family apart. We're all so close. Why fix what isn't broken?"

I shrug. "Good point. So you don't resent your mom for keeping it from you?"

"I did at first, but not anymore. She kept it from me so I could have as normal a life as possible for as long as possible before I found out and she gave me that. She and my dad gave me a great life—my dad, especially. He was my dad. I don't care what happens with Ron. I'll only ever have one dad and it wasn't Ron. My dad was the one who was there. He was the one who raised me and loved me. I couldn't be more grateful to him for that and knowing that he didn't have to do it makes it mean so much more. I love him for that and my mom was the one who gave me that. She gave me that by never telling me until she absolutely had to. I respect her for that."

I can't help but gaze at him while he talks. "You really think deeply about these things. I admire you for coming to the conclusion that benefits as many people as possible. It's honorable."

"I'm just trying to do the right thing. That's all anyone can ever do."

I'm just about to say out loud what I was just thinking about him being the best possible father for Dylan when Dylan lets out a massive yawn. I glance over to see him staring across the table at Noah, except that Dylan's eyes are glazed over and he sways in his chair.

I jump up. "Okay! It looks like someone is about to turn into a pumpkin. Come on, sweetie. Let's put you to bed."

He doesn't resist. He goes limp in my arms and stares up at me while I carry him into his room. He's already asleep except that he still has his eyes open.

He just lies there while I change him into his pajamas and he blinks extra slowly while I sing him his usual bedtime songs. I put him in bed and he just keeps blinking at nothing until I turn off the light and walk out of the room.

I find Noah sitting in the living room with his iced tea. "Did you eat?" I ask.

"I did. Now it's your turn." He gets up and comes back to the table. He sits down in the same place and sets his glass aside while I finish eating. "How are you feeling about....all this?" He waves at my house.

"I'm fine with it. How are you?"

"I'm happy about it. Thank you for doing this. You didn't have to. I'm really grateful."

"You don't have to be. You're great with him...and you're going to be great. You shouldn't doubt yourself."

He cocks his head and studies me way too closely. "But?"

I squirm and my cheeks flame under his scrutiny. He sees straight through me. "About us...."

"Yeah?"

I gulp. I've been telling myself for days to have this conversation with him. Now I don't know what to say. No, I know exactly what I should say and what I want to say. I just don't think I can bring myself to take the plunge and say it.

"Tell me," he prompts. "If there's a problem with us, I want to know about it."

"It isn't a problem. It's just...."

He waits for me to finish, but the words get stuck in my throat.

"If it isn't a problem, what is it?"

"You said....you said you wanted to build a future with someone."

"Yes, I did." Damn it, he really isn't making this any easier for me.

"You also said it was up to me how much you had to do with Dylan."

"It is up to you," he tells me. "It isn't like I could become any kind of consistent parent figure in his life without your approval. If you told me to back the fuck off, I would have to. I couldn't take you to court for paternity rights. The sperm donation agreement specifically states...."

"I'm not talking about that."

"What are you talking about?" he asks. "I sure wish you'd just spit it out and tell me. You're making me nervous."

Now I have no choice but to take a deep breath and say it. "How much you have to do with him is also up to you because it's up to you whether you want to build a future with me or with someone else. What exactly are we doing here? Are we just fooling around on the side or...."

His eyes go hard and unwavering. "Or?"

"Or....are we building a future together...in which case you would have as much to do with Dylan as you could possibly want—probably more than you want. It isn't up to me whether you do that...."

"Of course it's up to you whether I do that. I would never presume to tell you that I wanted a future with you...."

"Why wouldn't you presume to tell me? Why wouldn't you just come right out and tell me that you wanted a future if that's what you wanted?"

He cracks a grin and points at me. "Aha! At last we get to the crux of the matter. Why wouldn't *you* just come right out and tell me that you wanted a future with me if that's what you wanted?"

I look down at my plate. He's check-mated me so masterfully. He really is a thousand times smarter than I am. "Okay. I want a future with you."

"Look at me when you say something like that." He says it with a snap in his tone. He isn't asking.

I force myself to look up at him, but I can't stop my voice from trembling. "I want a future with you."

"I want a future with you, too. Can we move on now?"

I hesitate. "Just like that?"

He shrugs at nothing. "Of course. If you want me, just tell me. I'm all yours."

"What—just like that?"

He laughs. "Do you really have to ask? Do you think I've been going out with you and spending the night with you because I just wanted sex? I told you I wanted something serious. I don't want to fool around anymore. If I didn't think you were in my future, I wouldn't look sideways at you."

"So.....what are we supposed to do about it?"

He bursts into a huge grin and his cheeks flush. He holds out his hand to me. "Come here, baby." He pulls me across the table, kisses me, and then stands up.

He comes around to my side of the table, takes my hand, and leads me over to the couch. He sits down in the same place and pulls me down next to him. He props his feet on the coffee table and turns to me.

He smiles so broadly and all his features shine with so much happiness that I know it's true. He's wanted this from the beginning. He's been seeing us together since we first met. He might even have known it that first morning when he saw me at the daycare center.

He grips my hand and his eyes radiate so much love and understanding that my heart somersaults. Does he love me? Do I love him?

"Let's talk about how this is going to work. You said Dylan wouldn't notice me moving into your life because he's so young."

"I don't see that he notices. You're just.... there."

Noah laughs. He really looks gleefully ecstatic about this. "I guess I am."

"How do you want to deal with it? You're the one who's single. I'm here and I'm not going anywhere. How you move into our lives depends on you.....if that's what you're doing."

"What is the other option if we're going to build a future together—besides me moving into your life?"

"Us moving into your life...and into your house and all that."

"Me moving in here seems to make more sense," he remarks.

"But you just bought that property. You just fixed up the house and moved all your cattle onto the land. It wouldn't work for you to move in here."

He studies me for a second and then takes a sip of his tea. "Okay. How about this? I come over here every other Saturday the way I've started doing. I have dinner with you and spend the night....except that, starting now, I don't hide in your room until you leave with Dylan in the morning. We get up at the same time, get dressed, and I'm already up and out here eating breakfast when Dylan wakes up. He sees me being a part of your morning so he gets used to it."

"You mean...." I gulp when I realize what exactly he's suggesting.

"Then, after a while, I start staying over one night during the week and doing the same thing—having dinner with you guys, staying over with you, and going through the morning routine with both of you until all three of us leave for the day."

I stare at him as the truth sinks in. He's organizing our lives. He's building our future—the future we're both going to be living.

"We keep adding days of the week until I'm staying over here every night. We keep expanding until I'm living here. Then we can talk about all three of us moving out to my house."

I blink. "That's it?"

"Do you have another suggestion?"

"No."

"Do you think that will work?"

I nod, too stunned to say anything. This will do more than work. It's the perfect solution. Dylan isn't even three years old. By the time he's old enough to realize what's happening, Noah will already be a constant part of his life—a constant part of both our lives.

Noah cocks his head to one side and studies me. "Are you okay, baby?"

I can't stop staring at him. He's beyond anything I ever imagined. He's something so rare, something so fine and valuable that I don't know what to say.

"Come here." He hooks his arm around me and pulls me toward him. He kisses me, but this is nothing like the ravenous attack that usually leads to us having wild passionate sex.

It's passionate, but he doesn't lose control. He delves deep into my innermost being while his eyes search my soul for every ounce of meaning he can find there.

Am I really building a future with this man? How did I get so lucky that he would choose me? He wants to be the man in my life and he wants to be Dylan's father. Noah *is* Dylan's father. All the rest is just details and Noah is a master at those.

Chapter 13: Noah

Caroline moves in front of me and looks up into my eyes with all of her usual intensity. "Are you ready for this?"

"I don't think I'll ever be ready, but I guess I have to be."

"Do you still want me to do all the talking?" she asks.

"Definitely. They'll take it better coming from you."

She nods and glances over her shoulder. Dylan plays on the jungle gym occasionally calling out to her to look at him. He doesn't say the same thing to me. He completely ignores me most of the time, even when he sees me at the breakfast table after I wake up in bed with his mother.

I'm going to have to change that. I can't keep being a background feature in his life. I'm going to have to insert myself into his awareness, play with him more, be there to catch him when he falls, and expand our conversations so he starts seeing me as his father.

Today is not that day, though. Caroline catches sight of Ron and Claire coming toward us. "Here they come."

I don't trust myself to say anything. My last meeting with them went so badly. This one could be the explosion that sets off full global Armageddon. That would be just fantastic. That would be exactly what I don't need in a week of non-stop volcanic eruptions that have completely obliterated my life and put it back together again as something totally unrecognizable.

Neither of these people seems to realize that this is what's happened to me. They think this is all about them. Neither of them even asks how this is for me. They aren't my parents and Ron isn't my father. He's just some random stranger I got thrown into this mess with.

I don't want Dylan thinking of me like that. I need to make myself into my dad. I need to make Dylan understand that I'll always be there and it was just some trick of Fate that I wasn't around for the first two years of his life. I need to make him forget that it ever happened and I can only do that by being there every single solitary day from now on.

I thank High Heaven for Caroline. She's the one making this possible. I couldn't have prayed for a better woman, and what's even better, she's Dylan's mother. We're his biological parents. No one else can come between us and him.

Claire eyes me with some of her old suspicion, but Ron comes right up to me. He grabs my hand and presses it between both of his.

He gazes deep into my eyes and his face twists with emotion. "Thank you for meeting us. I don't know how to tell you how sorry I am about our last meeting. It must have been heartbreaking for you. I only hope I can make it up to you."

I don't know what to say. How can he make it up to me that his wife treated me like the most disgusting, shameful, horrible thing that ever happened to her?

She compresses her lips and doesn't come near me. She doesn't say she's sorry that her behavior hurt me. She doesn't seem to care at all about how this nightmare is affecting me.

"I hope we can get to know each other," Ron goes on. "I know I can't be the father you need me to be and I know you don't want me to be. I don't want to take your dad's place. I know I never can. I just hope we can be a part of each other's lives. I understand if you don't want to after everything that's happened, but it would be nice to get to know you. I don't want to think of you as a substitute for Hunter. I want to get to know you as a unique individual.....if you'll let me."

Caroline comes over and saves me from having to come up with an answer to all that because there isn't one. "I have something to tell you, Ron—and you, Claire. I had to do some digging for the Military—I won't go into the details about why. I had to contact the sperm back that I used to get pregnant with Dylan and it turns out that Noah is Dylan's donor."

Claire gasps out loud and I half-expect her to go into full hysterical nervous breakdown mode, but she doesn't. Her hand flies to her heart and her eyes fall out of their sockets staring at me and Caroline, but Claire doesn't melt down this time.

Caroline plows right ahead. "Noah and I are in a relationship. Noah is going to transition into being a father in Dylan's life and we're going to move toward living together and parenting Dylan together. I realize this might be a shock for you both, but it's what's right for us—all three of us."

A gigantic weight lifts off my shoulders when she says it. I couldn't have said it better and I was right. They take it much better from her than they would from me. I'm sure they would have gotten defensive if I just blurted out that I was moving into Dylan's life and taking over as his father.

Ron grabs my hand and squeezes it between both of his. "That's wonderful! I'm happy for you both. It's the best possible outcome, isn't it? Dylan couldn't ask for a better father. Congratulations."

Claire stands off to one side gaping at me with her mouth open. She doesn't even blink until, without warning, she bursts into tears.

She presses her hand to her mouth and blubbers loudly enough for the whole playground to hear.

"I'm so sorry!" she wails. "I know I don't have any right to be upset. It's just...so final. I always knew Caroline would have to move on with someone someday. I just....always hoped....it was stupid....I always thought that....as long as she was still single....Hunter....wouldn't be......"

She explodes in loud, heaving sobs and Caroline saves the day again. She puts her arms around Claire and holds the older woman while she dissolves in tears. Ron stands at my side and watches. Neither of us can do anything. This is all Caroline and she handles it perfectly—like she always does.

Claire keeps choking out broken words of apology and snatches of explanation. It all makes sense now. She didn't want Caroline to get with anyone else because it would be the one clear, irrefutable sign that Hunter really was dead and not coming back.

This goes on for so long that Dylan finally calls, "Mommy—look at me!" That's my cue.

I go over to the big kids' jungle gym where he stands at the rim of the giant slide. He still hasn't worked up the courage to go down it.

"Your mommy's busy helping your grandma right now," I tell him. "Let me help you."

I hold out my hand and he takes it. His hand feels so small, so weak, so helpless. My hand feels gigantic by comparison. Is this what being a father is?

As soon as he takes hold of me, he sits down on the edge of the slide with his legs hanging off. "You can do it, buddy," I tell him. "I'm with you. I won't let anything happen to you. Come on. I'll help you."

I tug his hand and he scoots a little farther to the edge. I give him one last pull and he slides down. I hold his hand all the way to the bottom and I whoop as his feet hit the ground. "Whoo! Yeah! You did it! Look at you—going on the big slide! You'll be climbing Mount Everest next!"

He bursts into a massive grin and rushes over to Caroline. "Mommy! Mommy! I did it! I slid down the big slide!"

"That's wonderful, sweetheart." She breaks away from Claire to hug him, but he only stays for a second before he goes tearing back to the big kids' jungle gym.

He scrambles to the top and I take my place next to the big slide. I hold out my hand and he sits down. He reaches out to take my hand, but when his hand gets inches away from mine, his weight pulls him down and he slides down without holding onto me.

His feet touch the ground. "Yeah!" I cheer. "Look at you go! You did it all by yourself! That's terrific!"

He jumps up grinning from ear to ear and rushes over to me. I rumple his hair, and just like that, he hugs my thigh for a split second before he races away. That instant of contact gives me a surge of power unlike any I've ever experienced in my life. I'm a father. This is my son. My life is changing. I'm changing.

I stay close to the jungle gym as Dylan moves on to other activities and taking bigger risks. He's learning and I'll always be here to help him and protect him whenever he needs me.

Claire startles me out of my thoughts by coming over to me and grabbing my hand. She looks up at me through watery eyes. "I'm sorry! I don't know what's wrong with me. I'm sorry! I know I shouldn't be....."

"Don't worry about it," I tell her. "It will be all right."

She nods fast and compresses her lips trying to hold back emotion, but she starts crying again anyway. Caroline materializes out of nowhere and takes Claire away.

Ron comes over to me next and I brace myself for another father-son moment, but he doesn't say anything. He just stands there and we both watch Dylan clambering around. I don't know what to say to this man.

I suppose that will have to come later. Maybe after we've known each other for a few years and we've had a chance to talk about every other insignificant thing that happens like the weather and how much Dylan has grown, then Ron and I will be able to have a comfortable conversation and we'll be able to get to know each other as men.

Chapter 14: Caroline

I give Dylan a hug, but he's already tearing out of my embrace and running into the daycare to play with the other kids. Willow takes his jacket, backpack, and lunchbox from me and catches my eye with a wild smirk. "So......?"

"So what?" I ask.

"I saw you hanging around at the park with that Hunter-lookalike. What's going on with you two?"

"His name is Noah," I tell her.

"Okay, what's going on between you and Noah?"

"It's complicated." I'll have to tell her sooner or later. I just don't want to do it now. "It would take too long to tell you."

"Dylan is going up to his grandparents' house this weekend," she points out. "Do you want to get together and you can fill me in?"

"Uh.... okay. How about Sunday afternoon?" I don't tell her that Noah will be spending the night on Saturday. I'll have to orchestrate this so he's gone by the time Willow comes over.

"Great." She gives me a hug. "I'll see you then. Have a great day at work."

She turns to hang Dylan's stuff on the hooks by the door. I rummage in my handbag looking for my wallet. "Did you get my payment for this month? I know I forgot to give you the extra activity fee for Dylan's paint set."

"I'll have to check on that. I usually check all my payments on the fifteenth of every month just to give everyone's banks time to send the payments in. Don't worry about it. I'll let you know if it isn't there."

"Okay. Here. Take fifty dollars for the paints and whatever else he needs."

"Fifty!" she exclaims. "That's way too much."

"Then take the extra for any other kids that can't afford it. Call it a tip."

She laughs. "All right. Twist my arm."

She takes the money from me and moves another step closer to give me another hug when I hear a loud screech of tires behind me. I glance in that direction just in time to see a massive truck come barreling around the corner.

It's driving way too fast and doesn't correct in time. It skids back and forth a few times, hops the curb, smacks a lamppost out of the way, and comes thundering straight for the daycare. "Look out!"

I lunge for Willow to tackle her out of the way, but there's nowhere to go but inside the daycare. I collide with her and we both go hurtling into the room as the truck smashes into the building behind me.

A catastrophic boom rocks the structure and then something explodes. I keep my head tucked down so I don't see what it is, and the next second, the whole daycare building implodes and a massive ton of debris falls on top of me.

I snap awake and try to jump up, but devastating pain knocks me down just as hard. I collapse groaning in agony, and when I open my eyes, I see that I'm in the hospital.

I immediately rocket off the bed. "Dylan! Dylan! Where's Dylan!"

"Take it easy." Noah comes over to me, sits down on the edge of the bed, and pushes me down on the pillows. "Just take it easy. You've been in and out of surgery for three days. Don't try to get up or you'll only injure yourself again."

I try to fight him, but my body won't cooperate. "Where's Dylan? Is he all right? Did he make it out of the building? Where is he? When can I see him? Did he get hurt? Where has he been staying while I've been in here? When can I get out of here?"

"Easy, girl. Just.....settle down."

I can't settle down. I try to push his hand off my chest, but as soon as I touch him, that feeling of his skin and body makes me look up into his eyes. The bottom drops out of my world when I notice that he has tears in his eyes.

"Dylan didn't make it, baby," he chokes. "The truck.....the building collapsed and.....five kids were trapped inside. Willow didn't make it, either. He's gone, baby. They're all gone. I'm so sorry."

Tears streak down his cheeks. I can't stop staring at him. He did NOT just say those words. "No," I tell him. "No, that can't be right. Noah...."

He doesn't even try to hide how devastated he is. Tears keep streaking down his cheeks while he looks down at me, but he doesn't say anything else. There's nothing more to say.

"No, Noah!" I hear my voice rising out of control. "No, no! He can't be! He can't be!"

He smashes his lips together, but he never looks away. His iron reserve makes this somehow so much worse—as if it could ever get worse.

"NO!!" I roar. "NO!!"

I try to shove his arm away one more time, and when he stiffens to hold me down on the bed, I attack him punching, slapping, and clawing at him. I hate him. I want to kill him for saying those words.

"NO, NOAH!!" I shriek. "No, no no!!"

He blocks as many of my blows as he can, and when that fails, he grabs hold of my wrist. He starts to wrestle me down on the bed to stop me from hitting him.

I fight harder, but he only uses his strength to restrain me. I feel him bracing himself for one hell of a battle. I can't fight him, and as soon as I feel him building up to full strength, I break down completely.

I burst into shrieking sobs. "NO!!! NO!!!!"

He grabs me and holds me. I feel him shaking, but I hate even that. My little boy. My son. Dylan can't be gone, but if Noah is crying like this, it must be true. Noah wouldn't lie to me about this. He would never, EVER say it if it wasn't true.

His arms give me a safe place to let out all the wretched agony in my heart. Nothing will ever be the same. I don't want to be alive with this feeling.

Part of me wants to get up and start looking for Dylan. All the old drive to go pick him up from daycare, drive him to my parents' house, take him home and get him ready for bed—he has to be out there somewhere.

He has to be right outside this room waiting for me. He'll be worried if I don't pick him up on time.

Noah lowers me down on the pillow and I see again the irrefutable evidence that it's all true. Dylan isn't waiting for me anywhere. He isn't worrying about me or hungry or tired or lonely or upset. Dylan will never need me again.

This ragged hole in the middle of my heart will keep bleeding and bleeding as long as I'm alive. No one will ever be able to stop it from bleeding. I don't want it to. I want it to kill me so I can go wherever it is that Dylan is waiting for me.

Noah doesn't even try to talk to me. He just sits there letting me sob myself into an early grave. He stops crying much sooner than I do, but no one could ever think he's going to get over this, either.

He doesn't look angry or upset. I'm not sure what he feels except that this completely destroys him. His old spark dies. None of the vitality and energy that made him so attractive is there anymore. He looks like he's aged twenty years since that day we spent at the park with the Jamisons.

That day seems like it was a thousand years ago and I push that memory away. I don't want to remember Dylan even as I keep obsessively looking for him everywhere. I want to get out of this hospital so I can go look for him. My mind won't accept that he's gone.

Noah snaps me out of my stupor. "Do you want me to leave?" he husks in a broken undertone. "I'll understand if....you know....you don't want us to keep.....building this future together. I know....it was all about.....him......."

I swallow hard, but I can't cry anymore. Crying doesn't do this anguish justice. Crying is so.....so outward.

This agony eats away at my insides. It turns inward and destroys everything I once loved about my life.

Losing Hunter was never like this. Hunter died overseas. My life didn't change that much when he just didn't come home.

This is something so deep, so poisonous, so destructive. It will annihilate everything, starting with me. I hate the whole world. I hate myself. Hate and poisonous ruin will consume my whole world until there's nothing left.

Noah can't even say Dylan's name. He waits for me to say something, and when I don't, he turns away. "Okay. I'll see you around. Call me if you need anything, okay?"

His voice breaks so hoarsely that I can't let him walk away. I grab his arm. "Don't leave." My voice sounds just as broken and desperate. "I don't know if....I can ever.....come back from this....but don't leave. I......"

I don't say I need him even though I do. I need him more than ever. He's the only person alive who understands this pain. I can see it in his eyes and in the grey, vacuous expression on his once lively face.

He used to be so chiseled and sharp and energetic. Now he's a shell of a man. I never understood that expression before, but now I see it in the flesh right in front of me. The outer surface houses nothing inside it. Noah is gone—slaughtered by the same crash that destroyed me.

The Noah that I fell in love with isn't there anymore. I loved him. I fell in love with him. I just didn't let myself admit it until it was too late.

Now I'll never love anyone ever again as long as I live. My capacity to love died in the same wreck.

He doesn't ask me to. I can see he feels the same way about me. Whatever we had is long gone and now we're both just stranded here in the same wasteland of broken dreams.

He doesn't hug me because there's no comfort for this. He doesn't move or say anything except to sit there staring down at me. His face is all puffy around the eyes and he glares out at the world like he hates everything, too. He hates me and himself and everything he once loved. I know exactly how he feels.

We don't have a future together because I don't have a future. He doesn't have a future. There is no future. There's nothing left except this rotten, disgusting, horrible, despicable moment. He and I have to keep living in it forever. We'll never get out of it.

Chapter 15: Noah

Caroline puts her feet on the floor and starts pulling on her clothes. I pretend not to see when she takes off her hospital gown and gets dressed. Her body means nothing to me now. I can't imagine why I ever wanted a woman.

I'll never want a woman ever again. I'm already dead. This purgatory of agony is just a waiting room before my body catches up with the rest of me in the afterlife of Hell.

I send my brother Tom an email while I wait. I mechanically go through all the routines of my business. I don't feel anything. Tom doesn't know about Dylan. He doesn't know about Caroline.

Tom doesn't know about anything that happened to me in the last few weeks. He'll never know how I turned into this walking zombie with no heart, no soul, no life.

Dylan. He came into my life for a matter of days and now I'm a wreck without him. My son. He's the only child I'll ever have and I never even got to know him.

I look up when Caroline starts putting her personal effects into a paper bag the hospital provided. She gathers up all the stuff from her bedside table. It's time to leave.

I stand up and put my phone in my pocket. Everything around me and everything I do feels a million miles away, but at least I'm still with her. She's the only person alive on this planet who knows everything. She knows what I'm going through. She feels the same pain.

She knows I'll never recover from this and she doesn't expect me to. She sees that I'm already dead inside and she doesn't expect me to be anything else. I don't have to pretend with her.

I see the same deadness in her eyes and face. She looks forty years older and all the loving, attentive essence that made me fall in love with her has blown away in the breeze.

I fell in love with her. I fell in love with her that first morning when I met her at my house. I knew then that she was going to be mine, but that will never happen now.

I don't even care about losing her. She means nothing to me because nothing does. The future is rotten and corrupt and poisonous. I wouldn't want to share that with anyone, least of all her.

She deserves better, but she'll never have it any more than I will. We'll both just keep on with this living death until we die for real. What a relief that will be.

She picks up her paper bag and mutters in a dull undertone, "I'm ready when you are." No spark of emotion creeps into her voice. She doesn't look at me.

I lead the way out of the hospital room where we've both spent the last week. I only left it to go check on my steers. I don't want to be anywhere but with her. Her presence gives me the only relief from this endless, all-consuming agony.

We head out to the parking lot and I open the passenger door of my truck without thinking about it. She gets in without a word and doesn't look at me while she puts on her seatbelt.

I don't look at her, either. I don't have to look at her to know that dull, hostile, resentful expression is still there.

I start the engine and drive through town. I head out into the country and drive her to my house. We both agree that she can't go back to her house—not yet. Pictures of Dylan, his toys, his room—reminders of him will be everywhere. She isn't ready for that. God only knows how she's ever going to be ready to face that. I couldn't.

I help her out and take her inside. I show her to a guest room upstairs and put her paper bag on the bed. "You can stay in here for as long as you want," I tell her. "You let me know when you want to go home and I'll help you clear out whatever you want to clear out."

"Thanks," she mumbles.

"I'm gonna go outside for a while. You can come and find me if you want to. It might make you feel better to get outside and walk around. You've been cooped up in that hospital for so long."

I don't know why I said that. Nothing will ever make her feel better. I've been walking around outside all week and it doesn't make me feel better.

She shuffles her feet and glances toward the window. "Uh...okay. I guess I could, but.... could you wait for me to change? I'll go with you."

"Okay. Sure. I'll wait for you downstairs."

I go downstairs to wait. She doesn't say the real reason she wants to go with me. She doesn't want to be alone, in this house or any other. She wants to stay with me. I'm the only person who understands.

She comes down in a minute wearing jeans, a t-shirt, and her sneakers. She looks so different from the real estate agent I first met.

She fidgets and avoids eye contact until we go outside. She walks next to me with her hands stuffed into her pants pockets. She follows me around when I open the gate to let the steers into the next pasture.

She tags along when I get my toolbox out of the barn and go out to the farthest fence line to fix a section of the water line. She squats down, pulls out a stem of grass, and chews it just like a country girl.

She gazes across the fields toward the trees along the creek. She doesn't say anything while I work.

I like having her here—as much as I can like anything. Her being here makes the world seem just a fraction of an inch less hopeless than it is.

I twist my screwdriver into the hose clamp, but on the next stroke, the screwdriver slips and falls out of my hand. "Aarrgh!" I growl. "Damn it."

"Do you want some help?" she asks. "Do you need a third hand?"

"That would be great." She comes over and sits down cross-legged by the hole where I'm working. "Hold this in place....please."

She holds two wrenches that secure the clamp while I torque the screwdriver with both hands. The screw finally backs out and I remove the clamp.

She straightens up and goes back to surveying the fields. Something in the way she chews her grass stem and squints into the distance makes me remember a few of her early comments.

"You never told me how you grew up outside of San Antonio," I begin.

"There isn't a lot to tell."

"Did you grow up on a ranch?"

"Not a ranch. It was in the country, but we only had the usual quarter-acre property. It was nothing special."

She brushes off my questions, but she sparks my curiosity. I've been dating her for weeks, but the truth is that I still don't know anything about her.

"So what was it like?" I ask. "What did you do in your free time?"

"There were ranches all around us. We used to go around and visit the horses and cows....."

"Who's we? I don't know anything about your family. Do you have any siblings?"

"I have two, an older brother and a younger brother. We're all one year apart so we grew up close. I was a tomboy growing up because I always went around doing everything they did. They treated me like one of the boys."

I have to stop working to look at her. Caroline—a tomboy? No one would ever guess based on how she looks and acts now.

I'm glad I can see her in these unguarded moments. She would never let me see this side of her at the fair...or anywhere else. She wouldn't let me see it at all if she thought there was any chance of it going anywhere. That window has closed for both of us.

"So how did you meet Hunter?" I ask.

"We met in college. I was studying economics and he was an engineering student."

Those words send a lightning bolt through me and my head shoots up to find her smiling down at me, but it's an unbelievably sad smile.

Is there some separated-at-birth reason that both Hunter and I studied engineering? Is there some cosmic reason why she was attracted to both of us—beyond just the similarity in our appearance? I'll probably never know and I guess it doesn't really matter in the end.

I go back to working on the hose, but now she's the one who starts asking me questions. "Do you think you'll ever go back to engineering?"

"I don't know. Running this place gives me a chance to make a living without dealing with anybody. I need that right now. I never could have spent the last week in the hospital with you if I was working as an engineer. Disappearing into this place and becoming a ghost sounds pretty good about now."

"Yeah, I guess you're right," she mumbles.

"What about you? What will you do? You won't be able to hide from the world if you go back to real estate."

"I know. I don't want to go back, but I don't really want to do anything else. I don't want to do anything at all. I don't really want to *be* at all."

I don't answer. I know exactly how she feels because I feel the same way.

"I know I have to do something, though," she goes on. "As long as I'm alive, I have to do something."

"Maybe you could help me," I tell her.

She bends over the hole and peers at what I'm working on. "What do you want me to do?"

"I don't mean that. I mean you could help me with the ranch....as a job."

She stares at me and her eyelashes take extra long to blink. "What do you mean?"

"The whole ranching operation that I run with Tom requires a lot of admin and paperwork and communication back and forth and bookkeeping and all that. It takes both of us working fulltime just to keep up with it. Maybe you could help us with that."

"But didn't you say that you have managers running your ranches for you?"

"They run the ranching part of it—moving stock around, sending stock to the sale yards, bringing in new young calves, managing repairs like I'm doing now—they don't do admin. Tom and I do all of that and it doesn't leave a lot of time to see the bigger picture."

The bigger picture. Am I looking at the bigger picture now?

She looks away toward the creek again. "You don't need me. I'm sure you guys are fine on your own."

"I wasn't thinking about it until right now, but it would definitely help. It doesn't have to be forever—just until you get back on your feet. You're already staying here. You might as well. It will give you something to do."

She shrugs. "All right. Whatever."

A lifting sensation passes through my chest when I think about her staying here and working with me, but that feeling vanishes just as fast. I feel like she does. I don't really care what happens. I honestly don't. I don't see anything being any better than anything else ever again.

I keep working on the pipe, and in a minute, I finish what I'm doing. "All right. I need your muscles again."

She bends down into the hole at the same time that I bend down to position the hose in the right place. Our heads bump together, and when we both jump back and look at each other, we both laugh just a little before we remember and stop.

We both bend over the hole more carefully this time and she holds the wrenches in place while I replace the hose clamp without any further problems.

I pack up my toolbox and she tails me back to the barn. "If you want to come to my office, I can show you a few things and you can get started."

"All right," she replies.

I take her to my office. I can hardly remember doing it with her on my desk and I definitely can't remember why I wanted to. All of that seems like it happened in another lifetime. That was a different man who did all that with her. I could never do anything like that now.

I show her through our ordering and invoicing system, give her access to our bank accounts, and show her the folders where all our spreadsheets list all our inventory on which properties and everything else.

"This is my business email account." I click to it. "You can see all these invoices that are awaiting payment. If you could pay those and enter them into the spreadsheet, that would be great."

She frowns up at me. "Are you sure you want me to do all this?"

"Of course. I sure as hell don't want to do it."

She shrugs again and sits down in my chair. "Okay. Whatever."

She gets to work, and when I come back inside from the barn an hour later, I hear her on the phone with one of our stock agents asking questions about an error on one of the invoices. I knew she'd be perfect for this.

Chapter 16: Caroline

Noah parks his truck by the curb and switches off the motor. We both sit in the cab and look through the windshield at my house—the house where I lived with Dylan for the last two and a half years.

Neither of us says anything for a long time. Am I really going to go back in there? I have to go home sometime. I can't keep living at Noah's house forever and I have to face the inevitable.

I already know what I'll see in there. Dylan's toys and clothes will be all over the place. Pictures of him will look at me from the living room shelf. His highchair will still sit by the table waiting for him to eat his meals in it.

He'll never sit in that highchair again. He'll never have to get used to Noah being there in the morning after he spends the night with me. None of that will ever happen now.

"Are you sure you want to do this?" Noah asks in a husky undertone. "You don't have to."

"I have to do it sometime. I can't keep hiding from it."

"All right. Come on. Let's go. It can't be any worse to see it for real than it is to sit here thinking about it."

He gets out on the driver's side, opens my door for me, and takes a duffel bag out of the truck bed. The bag contains all the clothes and stuff that I've accumulated in the three weeks that I've been staying at Noah's house.

I haven't had the nerve to set foot inside my house since the crash that killed Dylan, so I've had to buy all new clothes, a new hairbrush and toothbrush, and new shoes. I feel like an astronaut from another planet coming back to this place. Everything about it feels alien and wrong.

Noah takes my hand, but that hold means nothing now. At least, it doesn't mean what it used to mean. It means we're in this together. It means we're the only two people on the planet who know what the human race lost when Dylan died. We're the only two people who know the hidden misery of Dylan's loss. No one else gets it.

Noah leads me up to the front door and unlocks it with my keys. He pushes the door open and we walk into the scene I just imagined in the truck cab. Dylan's pictures smile at me from the living room shelf. His tote of Legos sits in the corner of the living room. His highchair waits by the table.

I wander down the hall to his room. His dirty clothes stick out of the laundry basket waiting for me to put them in the machine. His toys lie all over the floor where he left them. They're waiting for him to come back and play with him. They don't know he'll never come back.

I go back out to the living room and spot Noah in the kitchen. He stands in front of the fridge looking at some colored scribbles stuck to the fridge with magnets. I don't want to look at those. Looking at them hurts.

I rest my hand on Noah's shoulder, but he doesn't respond. My touch means nothing to him the same way his touch means nothing to me. Nothing can bring either of us back from this.

I go over to the sink. Dylan's bowl and spoon rest in the dish drain. His bib hangs by the sink.

"What do you want to do about all this?" Noah asks without turning around. "Do you want to get rid of any of this stuff?"

"I don't think I can. I don't think I can stand to get rid of any of it."

"You're braver than I am—living in a house full of his stuff. I don't know how you can stand it."

"It's better than getting rid of anything. I'm not ready for that. Maybe I still want to think a little part of him is still here as long as his stuff is here."

"Let me know if you change your mind." He turns away and grimaces when he sees the highchair. Every inch of this house is packed to the rafters with reminders of Dylan.

"You don't have to stick around," I tell him. "I'll be all right on my own."

"Okay. Let me know if you need anything."

He walks out without another word. He doesn't even look at me, and a second later, the front door shuts. Silence envelops the house.

I go into the living room and sit down on the couch. This isn't any different from those alternate weekends when Dylan used to go visit my parents and leave me alone in the house all weekend.

I can just pretend that's what's happening now. He's just out of town. He'll be back in a few days and my life will go on as normal.

Now I just have to figure out what to do with the rest of my life. I'm going back to work at the real estate office tomorrow morning. Helping Tom and Noah with the ranch was just a distraction until I went back to my real life.

Now I'm here....so what do I do? I don't have anything better to do, so I go into my room and flop down on the bed. I scroll on my phone and check out the new listings on the real estate office website.

I haven't been there in nearly a month. I don't recognize half the listings. I really need to get back on the horse before life completely passes me by.

I spent the first few weeks of this nightmare wishing it would pass me by. I didn't want to see or know or do or think anything, but that isn't possible. I need to do something even if I'm just going through the motions.

I spend most of the afternoon in my room. Okay, I spend all of the afternoon in my room. Anything is better than going out into the living room or the kitchen.

I go to the kitchen at six o'clock to get something to eat, but when I open the fridge, I find a bunch of moldy food waiting for me. Everything in there is more than a month old.

I can't face it, so I shut the door and go straight back to my room. I don't want to eat anyway. I get back on my phone and lose myself in mindless scrolling until I fall asleep.

Getting up in the morning is a whole different ballgame. I've never gotten up and gotten ready for work without getting Dylan ready, too. The silence sets my nerves on end, and after I get out of the shower and get dressed, I catch myself walking into his room to get him out of bed.

I stop dead on the threshold and my brain takes several minutes of staring at his empty bed before I can fully believe that he isn't here.

My throat constricts. I have to get him up. I have to get him dressed and feed him breakfast before work. How am I supposed to go to work if I don't get him up?

My heart rips when I turn away and walk out of the room without him. I go back to the kitchen, but that makes it somehow so much worse. I can't eat anything from the fridge and the giant gaping hole in my morning routine where Dylan should be gets wider and more vacuous by the second.

I grab my handbag and race outside to my car. I jump in and drive away, but I wind up driving to the daycare instead.....except that there is no daycare.

The demolished building slumps behind acres of Police cordon tape. The part of the building still standing looks like a monster from the Black Lagoon with the whole front of the building flattened to the foundation. No one has done anything to clean up the site and a bunch of horrible tire marks slice in a deadly curve across the front lawn.

I should just drive away, but I can't move. I can only sit here staring at it as despair and horror threaten to obliterate my brain.

Noah wouldn't let me look at that if he was here. He would make me look away and go do something else. He was the one who first suggested that I stay at his house instead of going straight home from the hospital.

He isn't here, though. He can't help me break the hypnotic grip this wreckage holds over my life. I might stay sitting here all day...or longer.

My phone chirps and makes me jump out of my skin. I scramble to find it in the vast bottomless pit of my handbag. My hands fumble when I take it out and I collapse back in my seat when I see that the notification is from Tom. He's asking me a question about the invoice I corrected from their stock supplier.

I send him a quick reply and I make damn sure not to look at the building before I put my car into gear and reverse away from the site.

I drive to the real estate office and park in my usual place. The rest of the day should be easy by comparison. Dylan never came anywhere near this place. I can get through my first day back at work without thinking about him.

I get out of the car, but when I head for the office, I spot Tim, Janine, and Paul standing around the reception desk. They're talking and laughing exactly the way they always do before work starts every morning.

I can't face this. I can't face being around people who don't know. I'm not ready to see their pained expressions or to hear their constant questions about whether I'm okay or their offers to do anything I need.

I spin away on my heel and stride straight back to my car. I don't know where I'm going, but I can't stay here. I jump in and start driving, but there's only one place in the world left to go.

I drive out to Noah's place and skid into the driveway next to his truck. I spot him out in the pasture near where we repaired the water line.

He stands straight and tall and unwavering with acres of farmland surrounding him on all sides. He looks like the quintessential cowboy—rugged, untouchable, eternal.

That's all an illusion, though. He feels. He hurts the same way I do.

I jump out of the car, kick my heels onto the driver's side floor, and walk out there in my bare feet. I don't even take the time to put my sneakers.

I walk right up to him barely holding it together. "I can't do this!" I gasp. "I can't do this! I tried, but I can't......I can't.....I can't....."

"Okay!" He holds up both hands. "Okay! You don't have to do it. You don't have to go back. Stay here."

"I can't...." I look around at everything without seeing anything. "I can't...."

I can't stop saying that. I don't know what's happening to me.

He grabs me and crushes me in a hug. "It's okay. You don't have to do it. You don't have to do anything. You're okay. Don't worry. You don't have to go back."

My brain keeps coming up with reasons why I have to go back. Am I going to be a permanent basket case after this? What will happen to me if I can't function anymore? I'll become a mental patient.

He pushes me back and holds me at arm's length with his hands on both my shoulders. "Look. You don't have to go back. You can stay here."

"But I'll have to go back sometime. I can't stay here forever."

"Why not? Move in here. You can move out of that house and move in here.... with me."

"But...."

Without warning, he moves in and kisses me. His lips and face and eyes look and feel the way I remember. They wake up all the feelings that went to sleep when Dylan died. I start to kiss him back, which wakes up those feelings even more.

I feel myself starting to get turned on, and a second later, his arms glide around my waist to pull me against him.

I explode out of myself and tear away. I retreat to a safe distance and pace around trying to kill that feeling. I can't handle that. "I can't! I wish I could, but I can't. I just......I just can't...."

"Okay. You don't have to."

I skid to a halt in front of him, and when I see the agony in his eyes, his face blurs behind my tears. "You should find someone else."

"I don't want someone else. I want you."

"I can't......" I feel myself starting to lose it. I try to pull myself back under control, but that only makes the despair well up even faster. "I can't......"

He eases closer and raises his arms like he wants to hug me again. God, I wish he would. I wish I could. Seeing him drop his arms without touching me hurts worse than anything.

"Move in with me," he murmurs. "You don't have to do anything else. I don't need anything else. You know you'll be comfortable here. Don't go back to that house. We need each other so you might as well just stay here. We're both a lot better off together than we are apart. It doesn't have to go anywhere. We can just be here together."

"But what about.... you said you wanted a future. You said you wanted to find someone...."

"That was before. I don't want that anymore. I just want to......"

I look up to find him looking away across the fields. "What? What do you want?"

"I just want to get by. That's the most I can cope with right now. I just want to keep going and I can do that better if you're here. I don't want you to leave."

That all makes sense because I feel the same way. He's the first person I turn to when anything goes wrong. His presence is the only thing that brings me back from the brink.

He takes the last step and plants himself right in front of me. He takes my hand, but as usual, it doesn't mean anything. It's so normal between us now that it doesn't bother me.

"Listen," he tells me. "Go up to the house. I'll drive into town and get your duffel bag from your old house and bring it back here. You can go right back upstairs to your old room and go back to doing exactly the same things you were doing yesterday before you went home. Okay? You can keep doing all of that forever for all I care. You don't have to do anything else."

"Do you really mean that?" I ask. "You aren't just saying that?"

"Of course not. That's what I'm doing. I don't see myself doing anything else. I don't see how I can. I just have to keep doing....whatever is right in front of me. Anything else is too hard. Shit, I haven't even told my own family about all this."

I can't handle this. I break down crying and I don't try to stop him from putting his arms around me. I'm too grateful for his chest to cry on. He kisses the side of my head, but it's all part of the same thing.

He understands. He gets it. He feels the same pain. He's the only person who does.

Chapter 17: Noah

I stare through the windshield at Caroline's old house. It's been two months since Dylan died and coming back to this place never gets any easier.

I puff out my cheeks and try to shake the tension out of my shoulders. "Okay. Here's what's going to happen. We're going to go in there and pack up all Dylan's stuff. Put everything you want to keep in boxes and we'll store it all in the barn. Everything else goes to the secondhand store. Understand? Beds—dressers—anything that doesn't have any sentimental value is going."

Caroline nods, but she doesn't look at me. She glares at the house from the passenger seat. She sits just as tense and determined as I do. This is going to be hard, but with luck, we'll get it done and we'll never have to see this place again.

"Let's go," I tell her and I get out of the cab. I open her door for her and then start taking flattened cardboard boxes out of the truck bed.

She gets out a bucket, mop, broom, and a bunch of cleaning supplies. We carry everything up to the front porch and go inside.

I stop there to look at the pictures, the toys, the highchair, and everything else, but Caroline doesn't stand on ceremony. She grabs a box, folds it into shape, runs a few strips of packing tape across the bottom, and starts scooping all the pictures into the box.

She works in a whirlwind without giving herself time to look at anything. She throws all Dylan's toys into boxes, tapes up his Lego tote, and moves on to the kitchen. She scrawls, *Storage,* on one box and, *Secondhand Store,* on another.

She starts loading dishes into the secondhand box and then kneels down to start cleaning out the fridge. That's my cue.

I go to her room and start breaking down the bedframe. We don't need any furniture at my place and she's already told me that she doesn't want to keep any of the furniture. We need to get rid of this stuff as quickly as possible so we can both stop thinking about it.

I carry mattresses, box springs, and bed frames out to my truck and drive everything to the secondhand store while she cleans the house. I make several trips to the secondhand store and then one to my barn.

I stack all of Dylan's stuff in a corner of the hayloft where neither of us has to look at it or think about it. Neither of us is in any condition to deal with Dylan's loss right now. We just need to put the whole thing out of our minds so we can concentrate on getting through the next few days with our sanity intact.

I make it back to the house to find her sweeping out the kitchen. The fridge stands with the door open. It's clean and she's unplugged it. "What do you want to do about the fridge?" I ask.

"Let's leave it here. I can sell it as a chattel with the house. Then we won't have to mess with it."

I nod and head into the dining room. "What about the highchair? Do you want to keep that?"

She shrugs, but at that moment, someone knocks on the front door. I realize a second too late that I left it open so I could carry the furniture outside.

"Hello!" someone calls. "Anybody home?"

Caroline and I spin around and my blood runs cold when Ron and Claire walk in. Their eyes swivel around the living room stripped of everything. The couch is still here, but that's it. All the pictures, the Legos, the coffee table—it's all gone.

"What the......?" Claire stammers. "What's going on here? Caroline, what are you doing?"

"I'm moving out." She snaps out of her surprise real quick and goes back to putting pots and pans into boxes. "I can't stay here anymore. I'm leaving. I'm going to sell this house and I'm moving in with Noah."

Ron looks over at me. "What's this all about?"

"Just what she said. It's too hard for her to come back here. We're moving everything to my place. She's going to live there with me from now on. If you have a problem with that.....well, I really don't give a shit if you have a problem with it. We're doing it. Neither of us wants to look at this house again."

I take one of the boxes of dishes from her and start taping it shut. Ron and Claire stand there gaping at us, but I'm so far beyond caring that I pretend not to see them.

I turn back to Claire. "What about the highchair? Do you want to keep it?"

"Naw," she replies. "Get rid of it."

I pick up the highchair to take it out to the truck when Ron dodges in front of me. "Wait a minute. You don't have to do this. There has a be a way to....."

I wait for him to finish. "A way to do what? A way to bring Dylan back? Is that what you were about to say? Were you about to say there has a be a way to turn back to the clock and bring him back to life? You aren't the one who has to live here looking at all his stuff all over the place."

I swivel around him and take the highchair to the front door, but I don't trust these two alone with Caroline. They just don't get it. Of course they don't. They aren't the ones who have to keep looking at Dylan's picture every day.

I get back to the dining room to find her taping up another box while Ron and Claire stare at her, slack-jawed. I take two more boxes of dishes to the front door, too, and when I come back a second time, Claire is trying to reason with Caroline—as if.

"Think about what you're doing," Claire tells her. "You're grieving right now. In a year or two, when this doesn't hurt so much, you might regret getting rid of everything related to Dylan. You might wish you kept his things."

Caroline doesn't even look at her. She keeps packing furiously and making the tape dispenser screech when she tapes the boxes shut. "You don't know what you're talking about, Claire. You really need to pull your nose out of my business."

"We're just trying to help, sweetheart," Ron tells her. "You don't really want to get rid of Dylan's highchair, do you?"

"Will you leave me the fuck alone?!" Caroline suddenly shrieks. "You don't have a fucking clue what I need or what I'm going through right now or what I'm going to regret in a year or two. Just get the fuck out of my house and LEAVE ME ALONE!!"

She hurls the tape dispenser across the room and it bounces off the wall. She blasts between me and Ron and takes off down the hall toward her bedroom. She hasn't gotten around to going through her closet and dresser.

I don't blame her for going off on these two. We have way too much work to do to waste time trying to justify our actions to two people with no stake whatsoever in what she does with her house.

Who the fuck cares if she gets rid of everything now and regrets it later? This is all just a bunch of stuff. The house is just another, larger piece of stuff hanging around her neck.

I don't tell them that we're putting Dylan's stuff in storage. They don't need to know that. They don't need to know anything.

I go over to the boxes that she was busy taping shut. I finish putting a bunch of dishes in them. "Look. Just get out of here, all right? You being here is just making it harder for her. Just leave her alone and let her make her own decisions. She isn't stupid. She knows what she needs a lot better than you do."

"We just want to help her," Ron tells me. "We're grieving, too, you know. We lost our grandson...."

"Dylan was not your grandson!" I counter a lot more harshly than I should. "You aren't my parents and you aren't more than acquaintances to Caroline now that Hunter is dead. You two have been hanging around her like a bad smell for five years. When are you going to wake up and realize that all your efforts to help are just making her life harder?"

I see them flinch at my cruelty, but I really just do not give a flat fuck anymore. I pick up a box to take it out of the house when a sudden crash of breaking glass peels through the house coming from Caroline's bedroom.

Ron, Claire, and I freeze and I look down the hall. Caroline is down there, and if she's breaking glass, she needs me. I don't have time to fuck around with these people anymore.

I take a deep breath to steady myself, especially when I see Claire's eyes tearing up. "Look. I understand you're grieving, but do it in your own space. Don't keep coming around trying to make a relationship with her or me into something that it isn't. My parents are dead and your son is dead. Dylan only had one set of grandparents and that was

Caroline's parents. I'm sorry. Now please leave. I won't ask a second time."

I put the box down on the dining room table and head for the bedroom. I don't look back to make sure they do what I said. If they don't understand that, then I'm going to have to pull out the big guns and they won't like it at all.

I find Caroline standing in her bedroom. It looks empty without the bed. She stares at the shattered remains of the dresser mirror and her bedside lamp lies broken on the floor in a spray of broken glass.

She glares at the empty mirror frame and her shoulders heave, but she isn't crying. She bares her teeth and pants heavily barely holding back rage. "I....I.....didn't mean to....." she rasps.

"It's okay. Don't worry about it. They're gone. They won't bother you again."

"I.....I don't know what I'm doing...."

"You don't have to." I take her hand and lead her over to the closet. "Why don't you go through your clothes? Divide them into piles—what you want to keep and what you want to get rid of. I'll bring you some boxes."

I park her in front of the closet and wait just long enough to make sure she's doing it. She starts taking hangars off the rail, checking each piece, and then taking out the hanger and throwing each article on one pile or the other.

I go back to the living room to find it empty. Good. Now I can take everything out to the truck and get back to work. Daylight is wasting and we still have way too much to do.

Chapter 18: Caroline

I get out of Noah's truck and squint into the sunshine at Pine Hill Farm. This place is good for the soul. I can actually start to think about having a life here. It calms me to know that no one expects anything from me here. I can just take it one minute at a time and do whatever I need to do to put my life back together.

Noah takes the last two boxes from the back of the truck and carries them into the house. Those boxes contain my clothes, jewelry, and other personal items from my bedroom. I didn't see him put Dylan's stuff in the barn loft. I never have to see it ever again if I don't want to.

I don't want to go inside just yet. I have a job helping Tom and Noah with their business. I have a house that is actually starting to feel like a home. I guess my life isn't as much of a disaster zone as I thought.

He comes back out, opens the driver's door, and takes a canvas bag from behind the seat. It contains tools and a few random battery packs and other stuff that I had hanging around my old house. None of it has any sentimental value, but we might as well use it here as anywhere else.

"You okay?" he asks me.

"Yeah, I'm fine. I'm just thinking. Thanks for dealing with the Jamisons."

"They needed someone to put them in their place," he growls. "They have no business offering their opinion on anything."

"Is that what you did—put them in their place?"

"Well, someone had to. I mean, Jesus! Who do they think they are telling you to keep the damn highchair? I didn't hear either of them volunteering to take it home with them."

I blush and look down at the grass. "Thanks. I owe you one for that."

"You don't owe me anything—as if they know the first thing about grieving over Dylan." He snorts and turns away. "I'm making steak for dinner. I hope you're okay with that."

He goes inside and doesn't come back out. I hang around outside thinking everything over. This place is so beautiful and soothing. It's a dream come true....or it would be without....all that other shit.

I have a hard time remembering why I wanted to give up on life when I see the pastures and the steers and the trees and the sunshine blazing in the clear blue sky. This place looks so perfect. It almost looks like nothing could ever be wrong with the world.

That can't be right, though, because there's plenty wrong with the world. Dylan isn't here anymore, but in a way, his being gone doesn't change how perfect and beautiful this property is. Dylan's death somehow makes it *more* beautiful and perfect—almost as though I couldn't really appreciate it if he was still alive.

I wouldn't be able to appreciate it if he was still alive because I wouldn't be living here if he was—not for a few years, anyway. I wouldn't have come to depend on Noah the way I have. This catastrophe wouldn't have brought us together like this.

In a way, he's given me something even more valuable than a father for Dylan. Noah has been there through the worst agony of my life. He's been there for every single second of it and he's shared it with me. He's been through Hell with me so I didn't have to go through it alone.

I owe him for a lot more than just putting Ron and Claire in their place. I owe him my life. If I can appreciate the beauty and painful perfection of life and nature after the Hell I've been through, I have him to thank for that. He's the one who got me through it so I can feel this way now.

I go into the house and hear him talking on his phone in his office. I only have to hear a few words to know that he's talking to Tom about some stock shipment that got lost when the truck driver couldn't find the right property address. Now two hundred head of steers are lost somewhere in the middle of Texas. I don't envy the two brothers for being responsible for that fuck-up.

I go into the kitchen and find the steaks in a bowl in the fridge. They swim in a marinade of soy sauce, chili, cracked pepper, Worcestershire sauce, and ketchup. They look divine, but I have a better idea.

I start working on the kitchen table rolling out handmade tortillas, and when Noah comes in half an hour later, he finds me cooking them on the stove. "What are you doing?"

"I thought you might like fajitas for dinner instead of steak." I shoot him a glance over my shoulder. "Let me guess. You eat steak for dinner a lot."

"Are you....seriously making homemade tortillas?"

"What else are we going to wrap the fajitas in?" He stands there staring at me for a minute. I flip another tortilla and then study him. "Are you okay?"

"Yeah. I'm fine."

"How are the steers? Are they on the right property yet?"

"Yeah. They're fine, too."

I frown at him. "What's wrong?"

"Nothing."

Something is definitely wrong, but a second later, he walks away and goes back to work. I finish the tortillas, cut up lettuce and tomato, take the rice and beans off the stove and the steak off the grill, and start setting the table for dinner.

I thought when I first came to stay here that it would be weird having meals without Dylan around. It turned out that the total change in environment solved that problem for me. I had never eaten here so eating here turned out to be a Dylan-free experience from day one. I didn't miss him as much because he wasn't part of my routine here.

Noah comes in while I'm bringing all the food to the table. I bring the steak over on a cutting board and start slicing it into strips. "Take a seat," I tell him.

He doesn't sit down. He comes over to me and takes the knife out of my hand.

"What are you doing?" I ask him.

He puts the knife down, turns me toward him, and starts kissing me. His lips tell me exactly what he's doing and my stomach tightens when a jet of adrenaline burns through my insides.

His eyes burn with all their old passion—and then some. A new lick of fire burns in their dark depths. I don't recognize it. It's mysterious and a thousand times more intimidating.

His tongue lights my brain on fire when it flashes into my mouth. He cups my cheeks steering my mouth into his, and without warning, he scoops one arm behind my back, crushes me against him, and digs his hard crotch into me.

I rocket away from him in a heartbeat. "Don't!" I yell.

"Why not?" He takes a step toward me, but I only leap farther away.

"Stop it!" I tell him. "We can't!"

"Why can't we? We've done it enough times before."

"It's different now. We just can't."

"That isn't a reason." He takes one more step nearer, but he doesn't try to touch me. He lowers his voice to a murmur. "I want you. I want us to be like we were before. I want everything we had before and everything we talked about when we planned for you to move in here. Okay, so it didn't work out the way we expected, but you're here now. We're doing it...."

"We aren't doing it! We aren't doing *that*! You said me moving in here didn't have to mean that."

"It doesn't have to, but I want it to."

"Well, we can't!" I spin away. I want to run from the room to get as far away from him as I can, but for some reason, I don't leave.

Feeling how hard and hot he is.... I shiver remembering it. I have all the memories I need to tell me how it will be if I give in to.....that desire.

I want him. I can't deny that. My body responds to him just as powerfully as it ever did, but I can't give in.

Feeling turned on by him....feeling that he's turned on by me......I can't feel that. I can't go there. It's too terrifying.

He comes up behind me and his low, husky voice makes the hair stand up on the back of my neck. "Why can't we? Why don't you want to?"

I gulp. I can't tell him that I do want to.

He places both warm palms on my shoulders and breathes into my ear. His hot breath sears down my neck and into my hair. His lips scorch my skin when he kisses the side of my neck.

"I want to get you pregnant with my child. I want to watch you grow and I want to watch you give birth to my baby. I want to be a father from the beginning and I don't want any other woman to give birth to my children. It has to be you."

He drops another burning kiss on my neck and crawls lower.

"You have to do this. You need to get pregnant with another child. You need to start building a future. We both do. You need to move on and start over exactly the way you did when you got pregnant with Dylan."

"I can't!" I choke down rising agitation, but it's more from desire than anything else—desire and fear of what he's saying. "I'm not ready!"

"Were you ready when you got pregnant with Dylan? You weren't ready. You were never going to be ready. You did it because you had to. You had to start living for the future and you have to start doing the same thing now. You started living again because you had to take care of him. You had to change his clothes and make his meals and put him to bed at night. Doing those things is what got you over Hunter's loss. This is the best way for you to move on and get over this one."

"I can't!" I squeak. I want to cry—mostly because I want him so fucking bad. He turns me on beyond belief, but the fear overrides everything.

"You want me, don't you?" he whispers. "You want to be with me....the way we were before. You're just scared."

"I can't do this!" I break out of his arms and walk away, but I still can't bring myself to leave the room. His presence holds me here. I can't ever leave him. I know that now.

"Why can't you? Turn around and face me. Don't keep walking away from me."

I turn around, but it still takes all my resolve to look him in the eye.

"Why can't you?" he asks again. "Why won't you let yourself be happy? You know it would work. You know having another child would pull you out of this. Why won't you let yourself do it?"

"I don't want to replace Dylan. I couldn't."

He lowers his eyes to the floor, and when he looks at me, he looks so sad that I want to cry. "No one will ever replace Dylan, darling. Neither of us will ever stop loving him and missing him, but having children won't make us stop loving him and missing him. I would love him and remember him even more if I had other children. Seeing them every day would only remind me of him. It would make me love him more and it would make it mean more. I would try harder and cherish them more because of him. He would always be first. No one could ever take that away from me—from both of us."

I clamp my eyes shut trying to hold back emotion. How can Noah say these things that I've never even let myself think? Every word stings, but only because I know he's right.

"I don't.....I don't want to do it with you because I have to," I croak. "I don't want to do it just to get pregnant. I want to do it because.....I love you."

My throat hurts saying that, but it's true. I can't go any further without saying it out loud.

He comes over to me and slips his fingers into my hand. That soft, subtle touch means so much more than his hot kisses a minute ago.

"I love you, baby," he whispers. "I love you more than any-thing—except for maybe Dylan. I fell head-over-heels in love with you at the fairgrounds and that feeling only got stronger the longer I spent with you. I thought I stopped loving you when Dylan died, but the truth is that I never stopped loving you. I kept loving you and the pain actually made me love you even more because we were going through it together. If I do it with you, it will be because I love you and I want you to be mine—always—forever—in every possible way."

I open my mouth to say something, but no sound comes out. I want to tell him how much I love him and how much his support means. I never stopped loving him. Going through this nightmare with him makes me love him so much more than I ever could have otherwise.

Knowing that I'm about to do it with him for the express purpose of getting pregnant with his child.....it somehow makes the act so much hotter, so much more powerful. It makes Noah magnetically, impossibly attractive. It makes me insatiably hungry for him.

I want to feel him pumping me full of his seed and getting me pregnant with his child. I want to feel him making me grow into the woman I'm going to become. My body aches for that future that he describes for both of us. I can't imagine anything more beautiful.

Chapter 19: Caroline

Noah takes my hand and leads me out of the living room. We leave all that food getting cold on the table and he leads me upstairs to his bedroom in the corner of the roof.

His bed sits under the gable with a big window at the head. Sunshine streams onto his bed and makes it look so inviting.....like a secret that only the two of us will share.

He turns to face me and I see my future written in his eyes. He's already told me exactly what will happen. We'll have children on this ranch. They'll grow up here with me as their mother and him as their father.

I can't envision a nicer way for kids to grow up. Why do I hold back?

All my doubts fade when I look into his eyes. I love him to the ends of the Earth and back. Nothing could possibly be worse than the last two months of my life. If he can get me through that, he can get me through anything.

He wraps his arms around my waist, and when he pulls me in to kiss me, he keeps his eyes open so we see all the way into each other while we kiss.

His hard knob teases me to raging, steaming desire, but that passion doesn't explode in wild, tearing animal madness the way it did in the past.

He rocks me there in the delicious knowledge that we're about to do it with each other. We're about to open our bodies to the future—the future where my body becomes the fertile ground to grow his children—our children. Nothing can stop that future now. It's just a matter of time.

He sways me back and forth in that knowledge for what seems like an eternity. I don't know when it will end or even if it will end. It will never end. I'll vanish into that future with all its fervent desires and pleasures and blissful moments.

We'll come together in this room every evening. We'll fall asleep together in that bed after we reach the heights of pleasure together. We'll wake up there every morning and we'll go to work.

We'll have to interrupt our intimate moments to deal with our children. That's unavoidable, but it will only make our stolen moments more precious and delightful.

I see it all in his eyes and in this room with the sun streaming through the window. No one can see us. We're alone in this little world of beauty and perfection.

He doesn't try to hide how hard he is and I don't try anymore to stop myself from feeling how much he turns me on. I want him. I want everything he shows me about our future.

I love him so much. I love what he said about Dylan's loss making parenthood mean more. I love that Noah understands that having other children will only make us love Dylan more. No one can ever replace him.

Noah moves over to the bed, sits down on it, and pulls me toward him. He doesn't stop kissing me while he starts pulling my clothes off.

This is all so normal and natural. Every move fulfills our destiny so perfectly just like every blade of grass outside is perfect.

He pulls me down on his lap and our bodies join in a magical dance out of the reaches of time. Nothing can ever be wrong ever again.

His body feels thicker, hotter, more intense as he builds up to the ultimate moment when it happens. He digs deep into the black inner essence of my being where he plants that seed that will grow into our future—the future we both need.

He rotates me onto my back and I feast my eyes on him rising above me in all his power. Nothing stops him from seeing the destination and taking both of us there. He's better than perfect. He's everything I need and so much more.

He lowers down on top of me and kisses me as we both reach the heavenly conclusion that will fulfil our destiny. His eyes never leave me alone. I don't want him to leave me alone. I want to see all his hidden power consuming me, claiming me, and turning me into something so much better than I've ever been before.

I can't hold back the tide when I feel him throbbing and convulsing in the throes of ecstasy. His seed floods me with possibilities and life-giving pleasure. That feeling rockets me into outer space and I collapse on him sobbing and screaming in delicious rapture.

He doesn't stop kissing me when he rolls off to one side. He stays between my legs touching me and exploring my body while he spasms inside me. My body swallows the last drops of his seed. I don't want to lose even one drop.

He gazes deep into my eyes. What is he thinking about? Does he see that beautiful future where we have a bunch of kids running around this property?

He suddenly bursts out laughing. "Are you going to make me Mexican food every night?"

"If you want me to. Is that what you want?"

"Hey, you won't get any argument from me."

"Too bad the food downstairs will all be cold now."

He smirks at me and gives me one more kiss. "We should have brought it all up here. Then we wouldn't have to leave this room for a week. Anyway, fajitas are just as good cold."

"I could heat everything up for you if you want me to."

"Naw. Are you ready to go back downstairs? Are you hungry?"

"For food, you mean?"

He explodes in laughter and I have to join in. "You're bad!" he tells me.

I blush and roll closer to him. I want to feel his body. "You keep talking about food. You must be hungry."

"I can eat first and then we can come back up here later."

"Okay. Whatever you want."

"Why is it whatever I want? What about what you want?"

"I want whatever you want. We can eat now and then come here ....or we can stay here and eat later. I'm flexible that way."

His eyes twinkle and he starts kissing me again, but a second later, he pulls off with a smack of his lips. "Okay. You win. I am hungry."

"Let's go eat, then."

We both get up and get dressed, but I can't help but smile at him and I catch him smiling back at me.

We go downstairs and sit down at the table. We load up our tortillas with fillings and he spikes a piece of steak with his fork. "This is delicious. Thank you."

"You didn't tell me if you want me to make you Mexican food every night."

"Well, we are both from Texas."

"But we aren't in Texas anymore."

"Was it really helpful for Dylan to always know what he was going to eat every night of the week?" he asks.

"Of course. Kids are creatures of habit. The more things stay consistent and regular, the more secure they feel."

He nods. "I know."

"I could change it up and keep it variable until the baby is born. Then, when the kid gets old enough to start eating solid food, I could feed them the same thing each day of the week and make something more interesting for us...or for you—depending on what we feel like."

He explodes in a huge grin when I mention the baby being born. It's happening. We're building a future.

His cheeks flush bright red and he pushes his food around his plate with his fork. "Whatever's easiest for you."

I slide my hand across the table to take his. I want to do a whole lot more than that, but I can satisfy myself with just holding his hand for now.

I'm going to have his child—probably several of them. All the questions of what our kids eat and when......Noah and I will have to discuss and agree on all of that.

Knowing that he's the man who will get me pregnant makes me want him again. I don't think I'll ever stop wanting him that way. Knowing that he's going to get me pregnant affects my body at the cellular level. It sets off a chemical reaction that I can't stop.

I could go over there, straddle his lap, and ride him until we both scream and gasp and collapse in blissful completion. I could take him again and again, but I don't want to do that now. We'll have plenty of time for that.

This moment, this sweet little conversation across the table where we decide about our future—this is the real pleasure. This is the most exquisite pleasure I can remember. It even feels better than sex.

It heals me. This moment shared with him in the privacy of our own home—it heals all the wounds of the past. It does more than heal them. It makes me something even stronger and happier than if none of those tragedies ever happened.

He squeezes my hand across the table while we eat and I see in his eyes that he feels it, too. The scenario he described in my living room—the one about getting Dylan used to Noah's presence—that plan was never meant to be. This was. This is the design written in the stars for us to come to this moment of ultimate happiness.

We finish eating and I clear the table. I put the leftovers in the fridge, and by the time I finish washing the dishes and putting everything away, Noah is nowhere around. I don't know where he is, but he's around here somewhere. He'll always be here.

I go out into the living room to wipe down the table, and when I finish that, I survey the room. This is my house. This is my home. This is where I'll be for the rest of forever—for the rest of everything that counts.

Something is missing, though. I want to do something more to make this house a home. Noah has worked wonders on this house, but there's something he couldn't do. Only I can do that.

I go out to the barn and climb up into the loft where I find all the boxes and totes of Dylan's things. I go down the stack reading the labels I scribbled in marker pen. Toys. Dishes. Clothes.

I come to the end of the line where I see the box labeled, Pictures. Sitting right next to it is Dylan's highchair from the old house. Noah didn't get rid of it. He kept it and left it up here.

Tears spring to my eyes when I see it. What a wonderful man he is. He's such a good father. Of course we don't want to get rid of the highchair. We're going to need it again very soon. He must have realized that before he told me about this plan to get pregnant with another child—our second child.

I run my hand over the chair's wooden sides. It's an old, vintage chair of turned wood with a carved wooden seat. I can imagine another toddler sitting in it, but that child isn't Dylan.

A chair like this was never supposed to sit gathering dust in a barn loft. It needs to be used, and if Dylan wasn't going to use it, I wanted it to go to the secondhand store so some other child could use it.

Some other child is going to use it. Dylan's younger brother or sister is going to use it. This chair could become a family heirloom handed down from generation to generation. Only Noah is insightful enough to see that.

I smile at the chair and squat down next to the box. I go through the pictures one after another. I hated them when I saw them on the shelf at my old house. Now they make me happy. These are the first pictures of our family—the family we're going to have. Dylan was our first child.

I select a picture of him alone. I'm not in the picture. I don't want anything to remind me or Noah or anyone else that Noah wasn't in our lives then.

Dylan laughs up at the camera. He looks so happy. He can stay like that forever in my memory. He can stay like that in our family's collective memory.

I chose a few more similar pictures, take them back to the living room, and arrange them on the mantel above the fireplace. Now this living room looks like a home. It looks like people live here—like a family lives here.

I stand back and admire the effect. It makes me happy. I don't need to call Noah to let him know what I just did. He'll see when he comes in and that's enough.

Epilogue: Noah

I come out of the house and carry a huge platter of ribs to the barbecue where Caroline stands in a white apron stained with barbecue sauce. She squints into the smoke while she flips burgers, sausages, and slabs of steak.

Ron Jamison and Emmette Hirsch stand nearby talking about something. "Hey, fellas!" I call over to them while I slide the tray of ribs into place next to the barbecue. "Don't you know barbequing is a man's work? You boys are letting the team down standing there while a woman does it for you."

Ron laughs. "You show us how it's done, son. You're the expert here."

I take the tongs out of Caroline's hand. "Move over, baby. Let a man take over."

She laughs and kisses me before she walks away toward the lawn where eight kids run around yelling and throwing frisbees and shooting Nerf guns at each other.

Four of them are ours and our two-year-old son Sam toddles around trying to catch up with the other seven who range in age from four to ten.

Two of the kids are Ron's and Claire's grandkids from Hunter's sister. The other two are Caroline's nephews from her older brother, Chuck.

I admire the scene while I take burger patties and hunks of steak off the fire and replace them with ribs. The smoke floats across the yard between my house and the barn.

Ron and Emmette go over to the fence and Emmette points toward the steers grazing and the creek beyond. Emmette lived in Texas for years. He knows his way around a ranch, unlike Ron.

The kids notice and run down the fence line toward the other end of the property. My oldest son Joe and my daughter Alice lead the pack, but the others break off before they get there.

They run over to the fence and the two oldest boys start scrambling over it into the pasture where the steers standing watching. Joe and Alice try to stop the boys from climbing into that pasture, but the others don't listen.

They jump inside and now they come face to face with several thousand-pound steers. They look a whole lot bigger up close without a fence separating them from the kids, neither of whom come up to the steers' shoulders.

Sam tries to join them, but Caroline gets there first. She picks him up, sits him on her hip, and says something to the kids in the pasture. None of them turns around to acknowledge her. They stand there frozen in shock.

Joe comes tearing back up the pasture to the barbecue. "Dad! Freddy and Wilson went into the steer pasture!"

"Yeah, I see that," I tell him. "Who do you think will win?"

"Aren't you going to do anything to stop them?" he asks. "Aren't you going to tell them to get out?"

"Nope. I already told them twice an hour ago. They didn't listen. Now let's see them get out of there with their dignity intact."

Just then, Shirley Hirsch and Claire Jamison come out of the house carrying bowls of potato salad, regular salad, pasta, and plates of fruit.

Claire's eyes pop when she sees the kids behind the fence with the steers. "Oh, my gosh! Freddy—Wilson—get out of there right now! Noah! You have to get them out of there."

I open my mouth to explain why I'm not about to do that when one of the steers turns around, tosses his massive head, and snorts loudly at Freddy, who stands nearest.

The two boys jolt out of their shock, stagger away, and Wilson falls flat on his seat in his haste to get away. The two boys scramble back to the fence and Wilson falls a second time before they both leap back over onto the grass.

The steer still stands in the same place. He never moves except to shake his head, flap his ears, and go back to grazing as if none of this ever happened.

Freddy and Wilson crawl across the grass to get as far as possible from the fence and the rest of the kids burst out laughing. Joe slaps his thigh and hugs his sides. Alice and her cousin fall over themselves laughing fit to burst and then the adults join in.

Freddy and Wilson look around them in a daze. I have to chuckle to myself at the sight. I warned those boys to stay away from the steers. Maybe now they'll realize that I wasn't just talking to hear the sound of my own voice.

Sam wriggles in Caroline's arms and she puts him down. He races off, and a second later, he runs up to me. He grabs the leg of my pants, tugs it to get my attention, and points toward the trees.

I bend down, but I can't hear him over the noise. I check the ribs and then squat down to put my ear right next to his mouth.

"I want to go to the creek!" he tells me.

"Uh...okay," I tell him. "Just give me a minute."

I make sure the ribs are okay and pick him up. I need to hand off the Sacred Tongs to someone. Caroline is free, but that would violate the Code of the Most Sacred Barbecue.

I flag Emmette, who is the only card-carrying Certified Country Boy around here besides me. I hand off the tongs, point him toward the barbecue, and he nods on his way over there.

I swing Sam onto my shoulders. "Sam and I are going down to the creek if any of you want to come," I tell the rest of the kids.

Joe and Alice come with us, but the others stay behind. They're more interested in Nerf guns than creeks.

I climb over into one of the pastures without any steers in it and the two older kids tail us to the creek. I put Sam down and he goes straight to the water's edge. He squats down, starts digging stones out of the mud, and throwing them into the water.

Joe and Alice start skipping stones and competing to see who can get the most skips. "Ha ha!" Joe crows. "That one did four."

"It did not!" Alice counters. "It was only three. You're cheating again, pal."

"Don't call me a cheat! How many skips was that, Dad?"

"I wasn't watching, son. Don't pull me into this."

"Dad can beat you at skipping stones any day of the week," Alice tells her brother. "No one can beat Dad at that."

"I can so beat him," Joe replies. "I got eight skips last Thursday."

"I don't believe you," she tells him. "Do you have any witnesses?"

"Witnesses! What are you—a lawyer?"

"Show him, Dad," she tells me. "If you can beat Dad, do it now. Go on. Prove it."

Joe glances over at me and catches my eye. We both know he can't beat me at skipping stones. If I stand up and join this competition, he's going to have to eat his words.

"I don't want to play anymore. I'm hungry." He runs off and Alice snorts at his retreating back. She knows.

She goes over to Sam and they have fun throwing pebbles into the water. She pulls out a rock, washes the mud off, and holds it in front of her little brother's face. "Look, Sam! Look how pretty it is! See the blue and green?"

"Pretty!" he exclaims and takes it from her. She hands it over and starts looking for another one when we hear a shout from beyond the trees.

"It sounds like your mom is calling you for dinner, sweetie," I tell Alice. "Let's go get some food. We can come back down here later."

I pick up Sam, but he's far too interested in his pebble to care when we start walking back up to the house.

The four grandparents and the other kids are all sitting down at the picnic table when we get there. Caroline circles the table serving everyone and trying to make herself heard over the noise.

Sam wrenches out of my arms as soon as we cross the fence. He and Alice race over to the table and wedge themselves in. Everyone is eating, helping themselves to the food, and talking at once.

There's no room for me and Caroline, but that doesn't matter. I sidle up behind her and slide my arms around her waist from behind. Her body moves against my chest and stomach when she bends over the table to serve Sam and Alice.

She doesn't try to break away, and as soon as she gets her hands free, she runs her palm down my arm to my fingers. She strokes my arm and a shiver runs up my skin.

Her engagement ring and wedding band flash on her ring finger. This is my wife, the mother of my children, the heart and soul of this little empire of ours. Everyone here loves her. She's the one who makes sure everyone here has everything they need. She's the one who makes sure our children grow up in the best possible way.

I bury my face in her neck and savor the quiver going through her when I kiss her. This woman is mine. All of this is mine thanks to her.

All of this turned out so much better than I ever could have dreamed and it all started with her. None of this would have happened without her, and in a few hours, we'll go home to our own room in our own house.

When all is said and done, I'm the one who will spend the night with her. I'm the one who will receive the full blessing of her love and I'll be the one she comes to for all the love and support and blessing that she gives to everyone else. I'm the one who gets to be that for her and that's the greatest blessing of all.

The End.

If you enjoyed this book, please consider leaving a review. You can also support me on Patreon at www.patreon.com/InvisiblePublishing.

Sign Up Once--Get all A.E. Moran's free books including brand new releases

When Doctor Lily Rice moves into a small mountain town to live in isolation away from the world, she sets off a chain of events no one could predict. Her arrival throws town doctor Parker Davis into turmoil. Is Lily trying to steal his patients and drive him out of practice.....or is there something much more sinister at work here?

The two get thrown together by circumstance and fate, only for secrets from both their pasts to threaten everything they've worked to build. Can two broken strangers find happiness through devastation before disaster tears them apart?

Sign up at www.authoraemoran.com to read it for free.

About AE Moran

A.E Moran is the contemporary romance pen name for Theo Mann.

I write 70 books per year—and yes, before you ask, all these books are my original creative work. Nothing written under my name is AI-generated or ghostwritten because I write better than AI and any ghostwriter out there.

People don't read fiction for entertainment or to escape from reality. People read fiction to see their humanity reflected in another person's character and story.

This is my promise to you. When you read my books, you'll see your own humanity reflected in the characters and stories. I take this commitment to my readers very seriously. My books are an intimate form of communication between us. I would never disrespect my readers by turning that over to a machine or another writer. This is my bond between me and you as my reader.

I write 20,000 words per day as my daily work output. If anyone with a public platform would like to challenge me to prove this in a controlled environment, feel free to contact me on this website's contact page. How do I do write so much? Find out more on my blog, *Crimes Against Fiction* at www.theomann.com.

I worked as a professional ghostwriter for fifteen years. Now I'm going for the Guinness World Record by writing 700 books over the next ten years and 1400 books over the next twenty years, all originally written by me.

See my website for the full book list. I'm also the author of *Proof for the Existence of God* and the *Crimes Against Fiction* blog.

You can find out more at www.theomann.com or at www.author aemoran.com.

Also by AE Moran (so far)

Standalone Novels

Heart on a Knife Edge

Dream Dimension

Just Friends

Back From the Dead

Damaged

Small Town Reunion

Series

Firehouse Blues (Books 1-10)

Turning Point Ranch (Books 1-10)

The Billionaires' Club (Books 1-10)